CW00675764

Steampunk International

Steampunk International

Edited by Ian Whates

with

J.S. Meresmaa (Finnish edition)
Pedro Cipriano (Portuguese Edition)

NewCon Press,
England

First edition, published in the UK July 2018
by NewCon Press

NCP 167 (hardback)
NCP 168 (softback)

10 9 8 7 6 5 4 3 2 1

Finnish edition published July 2018 by Osuuskumma
Portuguese Edition published July 2018 by Editorial Divergência

Compilation in English copyright © 2018 by Ian Whates
English Introduction copyright © 2018 by Ian Whates
Finnish Foreword copyright © 2018 by J.S. Meresmaa
Portuguese Foreword copyright © 2018 by Pedro Cipriano

"Seasons of Wither" copyright © 2018 by George Mann
"Reckless Engineering" copyright © 2018 by Jonathan Green
Characters and setting in "Reckless Engineering" ©2006-2018 Rebellion Publishing Ltd.
"The Athenian Dinner Party" copyright © 2018 by Derry O'Dowd
"The Winged Man Isaac" copyright © 2013 by Magdalena Hai, originally appeared in
the anthology "*Steampunk! Höyryä ja helvetinkoneita*" (Osuuskumma)
"The Cylinder Hat" copyright © 2016 by Anne Leinonen, originally appeared in the
anthology "*Steampunk! Silintereitä ja siipirattaita*" (Osuuskumma)
"Augustine" copyright © 2012 by J.S. Meresmaa, originally appeared in the anthology
"Steampunk! Koneita ja korsetteja" (Osuuskumma)
"Heart of Stone" copyright © 2018 by Diana Pinguicha
"The Desert Spider" copyright © 2018 by Pedro Cipriano
"Videri Quam Esse" copyright © 2018 by Anton Stark

All rights reserved, including the right to produce this book, or portions
thereof, in any form.

ISBN: 978-1-910935-91-0 (hardback)
978-1-910935-92-7 (softback)

Cover layout by Ian Whates,
featuring Steampunk International logo designed by J.S. Meresmaa
Internal design by Ian Whates
Text layout by Storm Constantine

Contents

Steampunk International
An Introduction

Ian Whates

This anthology has its roots in a meeting that took place during the Barcelona Eurocon, November 2016. Sofia Rhei, a highly regarded Spanish author and friend, had the idea of organising a small press symposium, where independent publishers from across Europe and beyond could meet, introduce themselves and discover what else was happening in the big wide world of publishing.

I had to leave the event a little early due to its overlapping with the launch of the *Barcelona Tales* anthology, but not before I had the opportunity to meet several contemporaries, including JS Meresmaa from Finland and Pedro Cipriano from Portugal. There was vague talk along the lines that perhaps we could work together at some point in the future, but nothing definitive.

It was with considerable surprise, therefore, that I received an email from JS the following July proposing just that sort of collaboration. The problem was that I had NewCon's publishing schedule mapped out for the next two years: I knew how much work would be required to meet existing commitments. I couldn't possibly squeeze in another title, could I...?

JS and Pedro's plans were already well-advanced, but they were looking for a UK-based partner to join the endeavour. How could I resist?

Steampunk: I had dabbled with the sub-genre in my own trilogy of fantasy novels, City of 100 Rows (Angry Robot), but had never ventured into the field with NewCon. Now seemed the perfect opportunity.

The first two authors I approached were obvious choices. George Mann and Jonathan Green are both successful steampunk authors here in the UK. George, in his earlier guise as senior editor at Solaris, had actually bought my story "The Assistant" way back when – the final 'professional' sale I needed to qualify for SFWA membership. Subsequently, he has gone on to establish himself as a respected author, particularly known for his Newbury & Hobbes series of novels – steampunk detective stories set in the Victorian age. I was delighted when George offered to write a new Newbury & Hobbes tale for *Steampunk International*.

I was equally delighted when Jonathan Green proposed writing a new Pax Britannia tale for the book. Jon is a frighteningly prolific author who has written and edited in a bewildering number of contexts, from Fighting Fantasy to Warhammer to Doctor Who and beyond, but he is perhaps best known for founding the steampunk realm of Pax Britannia for Abbadon Books. A new story featuring that dashing agent of the throne Ulysses Lucian Quicksilver seemed a perfect match for the project.

For the third component story I wanted somebody perhaps a little less obvious, a newer voice who is on the rise, with every chance of becoming as well-known as their fellow contributors. I approached Katy O'Dowd to ask if she would be interested. It turned out that she had recently finished a steampunk-tinged story co-written with her father under the pen name 'Derry O'Dowd'. Katy sent the story over and I loved it at once: a short piece that carries a punch at its moral core.

There we have it; a trio of stories that provide one leg of a tripod straddling a good portion of Europe – from the UK to Finland, to Portugal and back again. Steampunk with a truly international flavour.

I can only hope that you, the reader, enjoy the result as much as I have.

Ian Whates
Cambridgeshire, UK
April 2018.

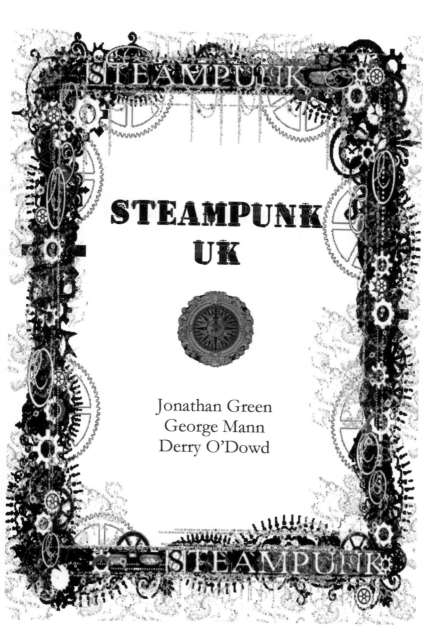

STEAMPUNK
UK

Jonathan Green
George Mann
Derry O'Dowd

NewCon Press

NewCon Press was founded in 2006 by accident. Intended to facilitate the publication of just one book, a fundraising anthology, NewCon now has more than 100 titles to its credit and has won multiple awards. Running NewCon Press has enabled Ian Whates, its founder, to work with many of the authors he has read and admired throughout his life but has also given him the opportunity to promote many new and exciting voices in the genre field. To some extent, Ian still sees the imprint as his personal hobby and continues to be baffled by all that it has achieved. To find out more about NewCon Press, please visit: www.newconpress.co.uk

Seasons of Wither

A Newbury & Hobbes Story

George Mann

Autumn

It wasn't much of a turnout. But then, Newbury considered, Alfred Wither hadn't been much of a man.

He eyed the members of the paltry gathering and willed himself to be elsewhere. It had been a mistake to come here. He ran his finger around the inside of his starched collar and adjusted his cravat. His skin was crawling, and the back of his head was damp with perspiration. His morning dose of laudanum was beginning to wear thin, and now the tainted cigarettes in his jacket pocket seemed to be taunting him with the promise of relief. He supposed he might have the opportunity to indulge himself once the small gathering had dispersed. He could find a quiet spot over by the far side of the graveyard, shelter beneath one of the trees. He'd need to, if he were to go before the Queen that afternoon. He'd need to quell his jangling nerves.

He sighed, and glanced up towards the slate grey sky. As if someone up there was working hard to ensure his morning was utterly ruined, it had now begun to rain. Fat droplets burst on the brim of his hat, and turned the listing headstones into slick, glistening fingers that reached up through the sodden earth, grasping at the sky. He reached for his umbrella. At least, he supposed, the inclement weather conjured the appropriate atmosphere for a funeral. In fact, the entire scene was draped in an aura of oppression. Fallen leaves formed a springy carpet beneath the soles of his boots, and a low mist still clung to the boughs of the nearby trees, imparting everything with a soft, dream-like quality; the perfect reflection of his dour mood.

Close by, the vicar was droning on about judgment and reconciliation – about love, and hope and redemption. Newbury wondered if the man were wasting his time. He wasn't sure a killer such as Wither could ever be forgiven, by God or man.

Wither had been a liar, a thief and, as it transpired, a self-proclaimed occultist of dubious merit; Newbury had encountered him on a number of occasions during the course of his investigations with Scotland Yard, and had been present during the man's unfortunate act of self-immolation the previous week, as Wither had attempted to summon some undisclosed entity of his own imagining, and had consequently set himself alight with a brazier.

Newbury had done his best to smother the sudden conflagration, but had been unable to save the man, and had been forced to watch while the flesh of Wither's face had blistered, and his outstretched hand had charred. He wondered if he'd ever be free of the sound of the man's screams, the stench of burning meat, the ferocity of the heat that had forced him back, his face buried in the crook of his arm for protection.

It was a fate no man deserved. Wither had committed the most heinous of crimes, and the newspapers had declared that justice had been served – but those reporters hadn't been there, hadn't *seen* it. To die like that… It was a diabolic fate. He'd seen similar bodies before, aboard the wreckage of the airship known as *The Lady Armitage*, and the images of their screaming, blackened faces still visited him from time-to-time in his opium-fuelled nightmares.

Wither had been a lonely, desperate, damaged man, and he'd died a miserable death. If he'd hoped to leave his mark on the world, he'd failed; the homeless people whose lives he'd taken would not be mourned or recorded, other than as entries in the ledgers at the Yard. Their stories would not be told. The newspapers had already moved on to other things, and soon Wither himself would be forgotten – another grim footnote in the history of a city already too awash with blood to notice.

Still, had he been alive to consider his final audience, Wither might have expected more of a showing than the vicar and two burly-looking men who reeked of gin, and had no doubt been former 'business associates'. And Newbury, of course, although he wasn't sure Wither would have entirely appreciated that.

Newbury was only present out of a sense of obligation – to bear witness to the burial, to put a capstone on the man's sorry career. If he were honest, he was there more for himself than Wither. He felt the need to draw a line beneath the whole affair. Something about the matter still didn't sit well with him.

He supposed the man had been a victim in many ways – his upbringing in the backstreets of Limehouse had served him badly, his only education his indoctrination into the ways of the pick pocketing gangs that plagued the capital's streets. He'd been a minor criminal for his entire adult life – a thorn in the side of the local constabulary, but nothing more. Yet his recent diversification into more unsavoury pursuits had drawn the attention of both Newbury and Scotland Yard, and there had been a string of suspicious deaths; corpses found in alleyways, drained of blood and marked with indecipherable symbols. It eventually transpired that Wither had been concocting his own, twisted mythos, and had been abducting and sacrificing homeless people on the altar of his imaginary god.

In turning over what remained of his home after the fire, Newbury and Bainbridge had discovered a plethora of charts and records, grisly trophies and notebooks filled with Wither's scratchy scrawl. In them, he'd detailed his ravings – accounts of supposed 'visions' granted by a divine entity, demanding Wither's allegiance. It had taken Newbury no more than a few minutes to establish that the man's entire belief system was the concoction of a fractured mind, bearing little relation to the arcane works he had studied – and continued to study – in such depth. This had come as no surprise.

What *had* come as something of a shock were the contents of

Wither's spare bedroom, which had been given over to become a studio, bristling with paint pots, discarded brushes, easels and, adorning every inch of wall, the most marvellous, vividly painted canvases.

Wither, it transpired, had been an artist of the very finest quality. His work depicted moving scenes of heartbreak and loss, of men and women caught in the very moment of breaking. In many instances the work had a romantic theme, depicting characters derived from British folklore and myth. Their faces were so incredibly lifelike, and they seemed to implore him as he slowly circled the room, seeking a solace he could not offer.

In at least half of the paintings, the female subject – a blonde, pretty woman in her early twenties – bore the same features, and had clearly been modelled from life.

Bainbridge had seized the paintings as evidence, and they had been carted away with all the other paraphernalia to be examined by the police, in the hope that, somehow, their contents or subject matter might help them to decipher Wither's true motives. Yet the haunting image of that woman's face had stayed with Newbury, and he found himself wishing he'd been able to converse with Wither, to ask him who she was, what she'd meant to him, and whether she had somehow played a role in what had eventually become of him.

He heard someone give a polite cough, and turned to discover that the vicar had finished his sermon. The man's thick, greying hair was now plastered down the side of his face, and he'd removed his spectacles in order to see through the driving rain. Four men in black suits stepped forward and, hunching low over the wooden coffin, each took the end of a rope, hoisting it up off the ground. They edged towards the hole and lowered the coffin slowly into the slick, sodden grave.

Newbury stood for a moment longer, and then turned his back as the men began to shovel heaps of soil atop the coffin lid.

They were down in the lower field, away from the graves of the more fortunate, where only the villains and destitute were laid to rest – those undeserving of a place amongst the holy. Newbury set out, boots squelching in the mud, keeping the church on his right, and instead heading towards the small cluster of trees in the far corner of the graveyard, close to the iron railings that separated the church grounds from the back lane.

The vicar called after him as he walked, asking if he wouldn't rather take shelter in the church, urging him to dry off and wait out the squall. Newbury simply raised a hand in polite acknowledgement and didn't turn around.

He waded through the mist for a few more yards, and then found a spot beneath an overhanging branch. He lowered his umbrella, withdrew his cigarette case, and struck a vespa, cupping his hand around the flame to stave off the rain. Within moments he was enjoying the familiar perfumed smoke, allowing it to trickle indolently from his nostrils. Almost immediately, he felt a flood of relief, and his shoulders sagged, tension draining. He closed his eyes and took another long draw. At least it was over now. He'd done what he came here to do. He could head back to his rooms, take a hot bath, and prepare for his visit to the Palace.

"It's a sorry state of affairs, isn't it?"

Startled, Newbury turned on the spot to see an elderly man standing a few feet to his left. He was wearing a heavy woollen coat, fingerless gloves, and a battered old cap. His cheeks were ruddy and sprouted white, wiry hair, and he was peering at Newbury from beneath bushy white eyebrows. He was holding a rake.

"I'm sorry?" said Newbury.

The man offered Newbury a sad, crooked smile. "Being buried like that, with barely anyone to mark your passing." He paused. "Friend of yours?"

"Not exactly," said Newbury. "Just someone I happened upon in the course of my work"

"Ahhh, now that makes sense," said the man, as if Newbury had explained one of the mysteries of the universe. "I'm Fred, by the way. Fred Ford. I'm the gardener hereabouts."

Newbury nodded, and extended his hand. "Gardening on a day like today?"

Ford shrugged. "I was out raking leaves when the rain started up. Had the same idea as you, I suppose. Thought I'd see out the worst of it here, beneath the trees." He gave a spluttering cough. "Sorry," he said, banging his chest with the side of his fist. "Lungs aren't what they used to be."

"You should go inside. Get out of the wet."

Ford shrugged. "I know. But there's another service this afternoon. And I don't like to think about the families, you know, worrying about the state of the place. It should look nice for 'em, when they're laying someone to rest. Like a well-tended garden."

Newbury smiled. "Here, then. Take this." He balanced the cigarette between his lips, and handed his umbrella to the other man.

Ford took it, his brows knitted in confusion. "But...you'll get soaked out there without this."

Newbury shook his head. He turned up the collar of his coat. "I'll be fine," he said.

"Well...I..." stammered the gardener.

But Newbury had already turned to leave, trailing sweet smelling smoke behind him in the rain.

Winter

"Where the devil have you brought me now?"

Bainbridge had huffed all the way across town aboard the ground train, and now, on the corner of Lexington Street – having left the soot-belching engine behind them – he looked fit to burst. He'd never been a man who enjoyed surprises.

"You'll see in a moment," said Newbury, chuckling.

"You were supposed to be helping me pick out a present for Miss Hobbes," said Bainbridge, with an accusatory jab of his cane. He looked bear-like in his enormous fur-lined coat, wrapped up against the wintery chill. "It'll be Christmas soon, and I refuse to suffer the same embarrassment as last year." The previous year, they had all gathered at Newbury's home on Cleveland Avenue for the festivities, and Bainbridge had made the faux pas of presenting Veronica with a beautiful, engraved silver cigarette case, forgetting entirely that she had never drawn a single puff of smoke from a cigarette in her life. Veronica had taken it all in good grace, but had ribbed Bainbridge mercilessly for weeks afterwards, and he clearly had no wish to repeat the offence this year.

"Yes, yes," said Newbury. "We'll get to that. We have all afternoon."

"That may be the case, but if we spend it gallivanting about, I'll end up in the same position, taking the advice of some darn sales clerk who doesn't know their arse from their elbow."

"Look, it's just up here. It'll only take a minute." He led Bainbridge along the street towards what appeared to be a small office building. He peered up at the windows. The blinds were closed. "I'm sure this is the right address..."

"Oh, so now you're not even sure where we're supposed to be," said Bainbridge, but it was clear he'd given up protesting.

Newbury carried on along the street a little way. Here, he found a doorway recessed from the pavement. A small plaque on the wall read: LEXINGTON GALLERY.

"A-ha! Here we are." He tried the handle, and the door yawned inward.

"A gallery?"

"Yes. As I said, it'll only take a minute." Newbury stepped inside, removing his hat and nodding to a young attendant inside the foyer, who gestured towards another door. Bainbridge bustled in behind him, cane clacking on the tiles.

Intrigued, Newbury wandered through into the adjoining room. It was a large, open space, well-lit despite the lack of windows. The floors were polished boards, and the walls were clean and white, and adorned with a vast array of vivid paintings of various shapes and sizes. There was no one else in the room.

"My God." Newbury turned to see Bainbridge standing in the doorway, gawping at the sight before him. "They're all by Wither. The paintings we found at the house."

"And more," said Newbury. "I read an article about it in *The Times*. The Lexington Gallery has been appointed by Wither's estate to dispose of the collection. It turns out there was another cache at a lock up in Limehouse, too. Apparently there's been a lot of interest."

"It's abominable. After what he did…"

"I appreciate your position, Charles. Really, I do. But then again…they are rather impressive, wouldn't you agree? I mean, just look at her expression here." He stepped closer to a painting depicting the blonde woman riding side saddle on a black mare, the wind whipping through her hair as they galloped over the moors towards a distant castle. She was looking back at him, over her shoulder, and her green eyes seemed to come to life, to twinkle with an unspoken secret.

He sensed Bainbridge coming over to stand beside him. "They're remarkable, yes, of course they are. It's just…I cannot separate the art from the man. He was a murderer and a thief. A vagabond of the highest order. The world is better off now that he's dead."

"And his art is six times more valuable, no doubt," said Newbury. He beckoned to the attendant, who was standing in the doorway, regarding them with interest. "I'll take this one," he said, indicating the painting.

"You'll *what?*" said Bainbridge. "What are you going to do with it? You're not going to hang it in your *home*, for goodness sake?"

Newbury grinned. "Don't worry, Charles. You won't have to look at it. I'm not about to hang it in my drawing room."

"Well, at least that's something, although I'm damned if I can understand what you see in it. I think it's the height of distaste. The whole lot of them should be burned."

"You always have been a harsh critic, Charles."

"That's not what I mean, and you know it."

Newbury nodded. "Alright, let's go and see about this present for Miss Hobbes. Just let me leave my card with the attendant, and I'll call back for this later."

Bainbridge muttered something vaguely conciliatory, and together, the two men set out into the cold afternoon.

Having seen Bainbridge into the back of a hansom cab a few hours later – following the purchase of a rather handsome volume of Keats' poems – and with not even the prickle of a potential case to throw himself into, Newbury had found himself wandering across town, enjoying the brisk, dry chill, and musing on the paintings he'd seen in the gallery that morning. He understood Bainbridge's reaction to the gallery's sale, and didn't necessarily disagree with him – the idea of trading on Wither's less than salubrious deeds as a means of making money from his art seemed distasteful at best. Nevertheless, there was something about the man's work that had struck a chord with him, and left him feeling as if there was something about the case that remained unfinished.

He certainly hadn't intended to visit Wither's grave – at least not consciously – but a short while later he realised he was wandering along the narrow lane close to the cemetery where Wither had been buried. He'd not been back since that rainy day of the funeral, and now the cemetery looked rather different, the ground covered in a hoary layer of frost. With a shrug, he ambled along the lane to the gate, pushed it open – eliciting a groan from the rusted hinges – and stepped through.

Today there was no service underway in the church grounds, and while the heavy oak door of the church itself was propped open, it looked cold and uninviting within.

Newbury walked along the narrow path that wound between the headstones, following it down to the lower field where Wither had been interred. His breath plumed, and he jammed his hands in his coat pockets to keep warm.

A man in a heavy grey overcoat was standing over Wither's

grave, noisily raking the hard ground. Newbury approached, his boots crunching on the frozen soil. The man looked up, and Newbury smiled at the familiar, ruddy face. "Good afternoon."

Fred Ford peered at him for a moment, and then his face broke into a toothy grin. "Oh, hello," he said, straightening his back and taking the opportunity to stop working for a moment. He leaned heavily on his rake. "I wondered when you'd be back for it."

"For...?" Newbury started, before realizing what the old man was driving at. "Oh, you mean the umbrella. No, not at all. Keep it."

Ford looked somewhat perplexed. "But it's a very fine umbrella, sir. I've been keeping it safe for you, like. Down in the potting shed."

"Really, it's nothing. I have others. Indeed, they seem to multiply when I'm not looking."

Ford put his hand to his mouth and gave a wracking cough. "Oh, excuse me. It's this damn cold. Gets me the same every year." He straightened up again. "So you're here to visit your friend. Only, you did make a point of telling me he wasn't really a friend, which is why I got around to thinking it must have been about the umbrella."

Newbury grinned. "Well, you have me there, Mr. Ford," he said. "Do you know who this man was, and what he did?"

"Aye. I know all of them what's buried here. But it ain't for me to judge, is it? Like the vicar says, that's the purview of him upstairs." He looked to the sky for a moment, his expression solemn.

"Well, I only wish I could be so generous, Mr. Ford. I was there the day that he died. I saw what he'd done. I was part of the team that investigated his crimes." He hesitated.

"But?"

"But I can't shake the notion that I'm missing something."

"Ah, well, clever chap like you, I'm sure you'll work out what it is that's bothering you. I always find the best way to find something is to stop looking for it. Whatever it is, it'll turn up when you need it." He stirred the ground with his rake.

Newbury laughed. "Wise words indeed. Well look, I'll leave you to your..." he trailed off as he considered what the man was doing. "You're out here raking, in mid-December?"

Ford shrugged. "Needs must. It's these darn weeds. Never seen nothing like 'em." He dropped to one knee and scooped up a handful of tiny leaves. They glinted in the sunlight, tiny and metallic. "They're tenacious buggers, I'll give 'em that. Every day there's more of the blighters."

Newbury leaned closer, peering at the strange growths in the man's palm. They were like no weed he'd ever seen – the leaves gave off a strange, coppery sheen, and the vine-like stems were twisted and threaded like steel cable. "May I?"

"Be my guest," said Ford. He stood, tipping his hand into Newbury's. Newbury poked at the odd little things with the tip of his index finger. They felt fragile and thin, delicate. He tipped them carefully into his coat pocket.

"They're remarkable. Do they grow all over the cemetery?"

"No, I've only noticed them these last few weeks. Mostly around the grave of your friend here." He grinned and met Newbury's eye. "I know, I know..."

Newbury smiled, perplexed. "Well, I'd best leave you to it. Thank you for your time, Mr. Ford."

Ford started to reply, but broke off into another coughing fit, and so raised his hand in farewell, leaning on his rake until the fit had passed. By then, Newbury had already disappeared into the lane.

Spring

"There. That should do it."

Veronica watched as Newbury tossed the newspaper onto the sofa and crossed to the window. He pulled aside the heavy drapes and – for the first time that day, despite it already being after eleven – allowed sunlight to stream into the room.

She winced, squinting against the sudden change in the quality of the light. "An advert in *The Times*? Really, don't you think you're taking this a little far?"

Newbury reached for his cigarette case, which was balanced on the arm of a nearby chair. "And why should you think that?" She could tell that her words had stung. She hadn't meant to upset him – but maybe it was what he needed to hear.

"It's just… it's been going on for months, now. We're worried about you."

"*We?*" He lit his cigarette. "So Charles has put you up to this, has he?"

"That's *not* what I said. Look, I realise what happened – what you saw – was upsetting, but this obsession –"

"*Obsession?*" Newbury threw his cigarette angrily into the fire, where it fizzled brightly for a moment amongst the logs. The room filled with the sweet stench of his favoured poppy. "That's not what's going on here."

"Then *talk* to me," said Veronica. "All you do is stare at that painting. I can't work it out. What is it that you expect to find in there?" She glanced away, unable to meet his gaze. "Is it the woman?"

"No, of course it's not the woman." He was pacing now, wearing a track in the old rug before the fire. "It's just that… something's not right. We didn't finish things properly. There's something left unsaid. Unresolved."

Veronica reached for the teapot and poured herself another cup of Earl Grey. It was far too early to be drinking afternoon tea, but she'd long ago grown used to that little quirk of Newbury's. "See, that's what I don't understand. You *did* solve it. You and Sir Charles. You worked out what he was up to, how he'd effected the murders. And you got to him, and stopped him. There's nothing unresolved about the case."

"I watched him burn."

"Yes, I know, and I'm sorry you had to see that, Maurice, but it wasn't your fault. You did everything you could to smother the flames. I know you did." She took a sip of her tea. It was lukewarm.

"You didn't see the look on his face, Veronica. I can't help wondering if it wasn't an accident at all." He'd ceased his pacing and returned to the window. All she could see of him now was a thin silhouette, both hands on the sill as he peered out onto the bustling street below.

"All right. Say for a moment that it *wasn't* an accident. That he'd intended to set himself alight. What then? How does that change anything?" She took a final sip of her tea, and then abandoned it, placing the cup and saucer on the floor by her feet.

"I don't know," said Newbury. "I suppose I want to understand *why.*"

"Because he was *insane*. He'd killed all those people, constructed a vast, intricate fantasy around himself and his actions. Perhaps it all began to unravel. Perhaps he realised it was all in his head, and he saw what he'd done. Is he really so different from all the other dangerous madmen we've faced?"

"But his *art*, Veronica. There's something about his paintings that I can't put my finger on. They're not the work of a madman. There are no pictures of this so-called entity he spoke of, nothing that relates to the murders – just those beautiful studies of human longing and loss. The two things don't correlate." He took another cigarette from his case and lit it.

"Have you considered that the paintings might date from before his psychotic break? That he might have stopped painting altogether once his mind had fractured, moved onto something else?"

"Yes, I've considered it. And you might be right. But I still think they're part of the story. There's something in those paintings that'll help me to understand. And I think it starts with the woman."

"Well, for what it's worth, I hope you find her quickly, and you're able to draw a line under all of this," said Veronica. "There

are other matters that deserve your attention. Other people who
–" She stopped short at the sound of rapping on the door.

"Come," said Newbury.

The door opened slowly, to reveal Scarbright, Newbury's
valet, who was wearing something of a sheepish expression. He
was a handsome man, younger than most of the valets Veronica
had encountered, and much renowned amongst Newbury's circle
for his great culinary skills. Newbury had poached him from
Bainbridge some months previously, ostensibly on loan, but had
so far refused to give him back. "I'm sorry to interrupt, sir, but
you have a caller."

"No, it's quite all right," said Newbury, stepping away from
the window. "I think you've rather saved me from a dressing
down." He glanced at Veronica, offering her a crooked smile.
Veronica rolled her eyes. "Who is it?"

"Mr. Aldous Renwick, sir," said Scarbright.

"Aldous! Well, you'd better send him up. And put on a fresh
pot of tea, would you, Scarbright. I rather fear we've allowed your
previous efforts to go cold."

"Right you are, sir."

There was a flurry of footsteps in the hallway, and then,
moments later, Aldous Renwick came crashing in through the
drawing room door. He was, to Veronica's mind, one of
Newbury's strangest associates – a rambunctious fellow of
around forty, who had the appearance of a much older man. His
hair was a wiry mess of grey and white, which stuck out,
untamed, like a wild mane. He was permanently unshaven, with
crooked, tobacco-stained teeth and yellowed fingers. His shirt
was open at the collar, and he was wearing a long, battered
leather coat, its pockets bulging. Most disconcerting was his left
eye, which had long ago been replaced entirely by a bizarre
mechanism, which fitted imperfectly into the empty socket,
protruding rudely, as if to give the impression that he was
permanently wearing a jeweller's lens. Deep within this artificial
eye – for Veronica understood that the mechanism provided

Renwick with some measure of vision — a red pinprick of light seemed to pulsate and glow.

"Aldous, welcome," said Newbury, striding over to greet his old friend.

Renwick slapped him heartily upon the back, and then turned to regard her. "Miss Hobbes. A pleasure, as always."

"Likewise, Mr. Renwick," she said.

"Come in, find a seat," said Newbury.

"No, I won't be stopping," said Renwick. "I just wanted to give you the news as I was passing."

"Is something wrong?" said Veronica.

"Oh, no, nothing like that, although I appreciate your concern." He turned to Newbury. "It's those weeds you gave me to examine. I've finished my tests."

"And?"

"And I've been unable to establish anything conclusive. They correspond to no known recorded flora. And that metallic sheen? It doesn't just *appear* to be metal. It *is* metal. Copper, to be precise. If I hadn't heard it from you, Newbury, I'd say they'd been manufactured, rather than grown. Where did you obtain them, again?"

"From the grave of Alfred Wither," said Newbury.

"Well, I can't quite fathom what's going on, Newbury, but those so-called 'weeds' don't appear to have any natural origin."

"All right. Thank you, Aldous," said Newbury. He had a distant look about him, now, contemplative and bemused.

"I'm only sorry I couldn't give you anything more definitive," said Renwick. "Look, I'd best be off. Sorry to be in such a hurry. I'm expecting a caller, is all."

Newbury grinned. "No, not at all. It's appreciated, Aldous." He guided Renwick to the door.

When he'd gone, Newbury turned back to Veronica. "Listen. Tell Charles not to worry. I'm going to get to the bottom of this, but it's not what either of you think. I'm certain that Wither was trying to tell us something; some message that we've missed. And

I'm going to find it." He walked over to the hat stand in the corner, and swept up his top hat.

"Where are you going now?"

"For a walk," he said. "I'll see you later."

The cemetery was busier than he'd seen it in months. People were milling amongst the headstones, spilling out into the pale afternoon from inside the old church. The vicar stood beneath the arched doorway, shaking hands with his parishioners, as they filed past, chattering amiably amongst themselves. Newbury wondered what it must be like, to have so much faith in something, to receive such comfort from it. He envied them that.

He was about to make a beeline for Wither's grave, when he caught sight of Fred Ford, down on his knees beneath a tree, turning over the soil with a trowel. He altered his trajectory, and walked over to join him.

Ford looked up as he sensed Newbury approaching. "Ah, good afternoon."

"It is, rather, isn't it?" said Newbury.

"You're back to visit your friend?" asked Ford, nodding his head towards the lower field. Newbury didn't have the heart to correct him again.

"Something like that."

"Well, I can tell you, he's been keeping me busy." Ford straightened up, jabbing his trowel into the soft earth by his knees. He looked red faced, and sweat was beading on his forehead. He spluttered, and reached into his pocket for a handkerchief. The spluttering gave way to a fierce, wracking cough.

"Are you quite well?" said Newbury, redundantly. "Do you need any assistance? That cough has been lingering since last winter."

Ford waved his hand dismissively. "No, no. I'll be fine. Nothing to worry about." His voice was a dry croak.

Newbury reached into his jacket and withdrew a small silver

hip flask. He unscrewed the cap, and handed it to Ford. "Here, take a nip of that. Might help."

Ford grinned up at him, then winked, before taking the proffered flask and downing a long draw. He handed it back to Newbury, and then wiped his mouth on his sleeve. "Much obliged to you."

"You were saying? About Alfred Wither keeping you busy. Has he had a lot of visitors?"

"Oh, no, nothing like that. I should say you're the only one who's come by his grave since he was interred down here, to be honest with you. No, it's those bloomin' weeds. Bane of my life, they are. No sooner have I cleared 'em up, then they're back again. Took a load out this morning, too."

"Yes, I've been wondering about those. I had a friend of mine take a look at the samples you gave me. He says they bear no resemblance to any known flora he can find."

"Darn right," said Ford. "I ain't never seen anything like it."

"Have they spread?" said Newbury.

Ford shook his head. "No, but then, I've kept on top of 'em. Once a day I take a trip down there and clear them up. There's always new shoots, that's the thing, glinting in the sunlight. But I keep it nice, like. He might have been a bad man in his time, but all is equal in the end, when they're six feet under. Toffs and vagabonds alike."

"You're a good man, Mr. Ford," said Newbury.

"Aye, well, I'll be in for a good rollicking off the vicar if I don't press on. Been nice seeing you again, sir. I've kept that umbrella nice. You can be sure of that."

"I don't doubt it," said Newbury. "Until next time."

He left Ford to return to his work, and meandered down to Wither's grave, but there was nothing to see. Ford had been true to his word — the ground had been well tended, and there was no sign of the metallic shoots that he'd come to see.

With a heavy sigh, he quit the graveyard for the long walk home.

Summer

The breeze from the open window was pleasant upon the back of his neck, but the sound of the street below was a constant distraction, not to mention the distant chugging of ground trains, the trilling of bicycle bells, and the indecipherable call of newspaper salesmen.

Newbury rose to his feet, crossed the room, and slammed the window down in its frame. Immediately, the room was washed in blissful silence. He supposed he'd be able to manage another half hour of the stifling heat before he had to open it again.

He slumped back into his chair, only to knock his book off the arm, sending it tumbling to the rug, where it promptly snapped shut, losing his page. He issued a frustrated groan. He abhorred the heat. London wasn't equipped for it. He'd felt differently in India, where the clothes, the buildings and the culture had been designed to accommodate it, but here, in his drawing room, the heat made him feel sluggish and uncomfortable.

He leaned over to collect his book. There was a rap at the front door. He sat back in his chair. The last thing he wanted now was a visitor.

Scarbright's footsteps followed, along with the murmuring tones of another man. The drawing room door creaked open.

"You have a caller, sir."

"I'm not receiving callers today, Scarbright."

"Only, it's a gentleman who says he's responding to your advert in *The Times*."

Newbury sat forward, peering inquisitively at Scarbright. His advert in *The Times*? The only recent advert had been months ago, regarding the woman in Wither's paintings. He got to his feet, smoothing the front of his crumpled shirt. "Well, I suppose you'd better show him in, then."

"Very good, sir."

Newbury hurriedly grabbed his ashtray from the sofa and

brushed away the spilt ash. Moments later, the gentleman in question was shown through by Scarbright. He was a stocky fellow, clean-shaven, with startling green eyes and hair the colour of Saharan sand. He wore a smart black suit, his collar fastened despite the weather, and as he handed Scarbright his hat, Newbury caught a glimpse of deeply ingrained ink smudges on the side of his right hand. A clerk, then.

"Welcome, Mr...?"

"Merrison, sir. Clifford Merrison." His voice was a little tremulous, and his eyes were flitting about the place, betraying his nerves.

"Well, Mr. Merrison, why don't you take a seat? Can I offer you a cigarette?"

"No, thank you," said Merrison. He took the proffered seat on the sofa, but sat on the very edge of the cushion, as if he dared not relax. Newbury turned his armchair about to face the man, then sat opposite, reaching for his cigarettes.

"You're here about my advert in *The Times*?"

"Yes. I'm sorry it's taken so long. The thing is, you see, I've hesitated about coming to see you."

"And why is that, Mr. Merrison?"

"Because the woman in the paintings is my sister."

Newbury leaned forward in his chair. "Your sister? Where is she now?"

"The cemetery at St. Bartholomew's, if you know it?"

"I know it well. I'm sorry for your loss." Newbury paused, weighing his next words with care. "Might I ask...was Alfred Wither responsible for her death?"

"Oh, good lord, no. Alfred was always a good man. He and Charlotte were engaged to be married. He treated her with the greatest respect. We all adored him, for all his quirks. Had a bit of an artistic temperament, of course, but that's only to be expected."

"You're aware of what he did, I presume? What became of him?"

Merrison nodded. "Yes. I regret that I was unable to attend

his funeral, but Father and I… we're trying to protect Lottie, you see. We didn't want her name being dragged through the newspapers. She wasn't a part of what happened to Alfred, and if he'd been in his right mind, he wouldn't have wanted her associated with all of that."

"So you agree that he wasn't in his right mind at the time of his death?"

Merrison shook his head. "No. He was deeply affected by what happened to Lottie. I think it pushed him over the edge, caused his mind to fracture. All that stuff about divine spirits and the afterlife – I think that was his way of trying to find a way to bring her back. That's how he coped with it all. Or rather, that's how he *tried* to cope."

So *that* was the connection. That was what Wither had been doing – seeking ways to restore his lost love. He must have suffered tremendously after her loss. "What became of Charlotte?" said Newbury. "What happened to send him so far over the precipice?"

"I fear the burden of her death rests upon my shoulders, Sir Maurice. I'd taken out a higher purchase contract on an automaton from Chapman & Villiers. I'm not sure if you recall the scandal from a few years ago – scores of their automata became crazed, attacking their human masters?"

Newbury could hardly believe what he was hearing. He'd considered the Chapman & Villiers affair long put to rest, but now here was a young man, sitting on his sofa all this time later, explaining how the repercussions of that sorry business were still being felt. "Yes," he said, his voice level. "I'm aware of the matter."

Merrison nodded. "Father had thrown a party to celebrate my new position at the bank – I'm a clerk, you see – and we'd all gathered at the family home. Alfred was there, too, along with a few of his and Lottie's friends. There was no warning; no sign that anything untoward was about to occur. One minute the automaton was fetching a tray of drinks from the kitchen – the next it had taken hold of Lottie and torn out her throat." He lowered his head as he spoke, choked with emotion, so that he had to fight to get the words out. "We stopped it, of course. Pinned it down and destroyed it, but it was too late for Lottie. She was already dead. We all saw it happen, right there in front of us. None of us have been the same since."

"I don't doubt it," said Newbury, gently. "And it's after that, that Wither became unhinged?"

"Yes. He stopped visiting. Couldn't come near the house, because of the memories it evoked. It was all too raw. He didn't want to see any of us. We tried calling on him, but he had taken to his bed. He refused to answer the door. We sent a doctor round, but even he couldn't get over the threshold. Then we heard he'd taken up with some spiritualist, and at the time we were relieved. None of us had ever put much stock in that sort of thing, but at least he was talking to someone. Little did we know that he'd already started to concoct his strange fantasies."

"And that was the last you or your family had to do with him?"

"I saw him once after that, on Charing Cross Road. He was coming out of a bookshop. He looked feverish and unkempt. I tried to intercept him, to ask if he needed anything, but he simply muttered something about a great piece of art he was working on, and brushed me aside as if he barely knew me." Merrison met Newbury's gaze. "I realise now that I might have done something. If I'd only stopped him..."

"You cannot blame yourself," said Newbury. "If anything, the original fault lies with Chapman & Villiers. You put your trust in them, and they failed you. You couldn't have known what would happen to Wither."

"I see that you are a generous man, Sir Maurice, and so I shall prevail on your kindness. Please, do not in any way associate my family or my sister's name with the horrors committed by Alfred. It would be the end of us. We've already had to bear so much."

Newbury nodded. "You have my word. And thank you, Mr. Merrison, for answering my call, and settling the matter in my mind. I had thought there unfinished business, and I see now that it is best left undisturbed. Alfred Wither died of a broken heart, and there is no more to be said."

Merrison got to his feet. "My thanks to you, Sir Maurice." He took Newbury's hand and pumped it firmly. "And now I have discharged my duty. I shall take my leave."

Newbury walked him to the door. "Before you go, I think there's something you should have." He ducked back into the drawing room and collected a picture frame that he'd propped against the bookshelves. "Here." He held the painting out to Merrison.

Merrison looked completely taken aback. Tears pricked his eyes at the sight of his sister, glancing back at him over her shoulder as she galloped across the moors towards her distant castle. She looked as if she were smiling up at him. "Oh, but Sir Maurice – I can't."

"Please. It belongs to you."

Merrison accepted the frame. He swallowed. "You're a kind man, Sir Maurice," he said. "Goodbye." He ducked out into the hall, daubing his eyes with his sleeve, and a moment later Newbury heard the front door close behind him.

The heat was finally beginning to subside as Newbury made his way along the narrow lane towards the cemetery later that afternoon. The sun was dipping low over the horizon, casting everything in a warm, coppery glow, and the streets were still bustling with folk making the most of the clement weather. Children chased each other and played ball, while others sat out on their doorsteps, sipping drinks and chattering.

The graveyard itself was quiet, and as Newbury closed the creaking gate behind him, he noticed immediately that something had changed. The grass between the headstones was long and overgrown, and speckled with daisies and dandelion heads. It was even beginning to encroach on the path, where previously there had always been a neat and formal division.

He glanced around, searching for any sign of Fred Ford. He was nowhere to be seen. He heard someone cough, and for a moment thought it must have been Ford, over by the church, but it was only the vicar, clearing his throat as he came along the path to greet him.

"Good evening, sir. May I be of assistance? You look a little lost."

Newbury smiled. "I was looking for Fred. Fred Ford. Is he not working today?"

"Ahh," the vicar's expression became suddenly solemn. "He said you might be along. I presume you're the gentleman who loaned him your umbrella?"

"That's right," said Newbury.

The vicar nodded. "I'm afraid I have some rather sombre news. Fred passed away three weeks ago. An affliction of the lungs."

"Oh...I..." Newbury trailed off, unsure what to say. He'd come to view the old man as something of a fixture.

"I gather the two of you were friends."

"Well..." Newbury started to correct the man, but then caught himself, and smiled. "Yes, we were friends."

"Then I'm sorry for your loss. He was a good man. He cherished your gift, you know. Used to talk about it often."

Newbury frowned. "But it was only an umbrella."

The vicar grinned. "What might have seemed like a trifle to you, sir, meant more to an old man than you could imagine. Often, when we give someone a gift, we give them more than the gift itself."

Newbury nodded. "He'll be missed."

"Indeed. And soon I shall have to advertise for a new gardener. It's only when someone is no longer there that we truly see how much they contributed. The cemetery was always so well tended."

"Well, allow me to make a small donation to the church coffers. Perhaps you could use some of it to ensure Mr. Ford is remembered." Newbury reached for his wallet and withdrew a couple of notes, which he handed to the vicar.

"That's really most generous of you, Mr...?"

"Newbury. Sir Maurice Newbury."

"I'm sure Fred would appreciate it, Sir Maurice. Now, is there anything else I can do for you? I can pop the kettle on in the church if you're in need of a restorative?"

Newbury shook his head. "No, thank you. There's someone else I'm hoping to look in on while I'm here."

"Ah, yes. Down in the lower field. It seems like only yesterday since the funeral. A miserable affair, indeed. But good of you to pay your respects."

"As Fred used to say, it's not our place to judge."

"True enough," said the vicar. "Then good day to you, sir, and my thanks for your generosity."

Newbury touched the brim of his hat, and set off down the path towards the lower field.

Here, the grass had run even more rampant, the graves left untended for weeks on end. Fred would have been distraught to see it in such a wild state, but Newbury felt there was something appropriate in it; the return to nature, the giving over of the body to the earth.

As he approached, he caught sight of something glinting in the waning sunlight: a twisted, shimmering eruption of stems and leaves. This, he realised, was Wither's grave run wild, abandoned after Ford's death, the weeds left to flourish.

He picked up his pace, breaking into a slow jog. Sweat trickled down the crease of his back. As he drew closer, he saw the true scale of the growth – it towered over him, ten, twelve feet tall. It was pillar-like, rising up in a straight column, perfectly unnatural, and yet retaining its odd, organic design. Wither's small, unadorned headstone had been completely smothered by it.

Newbury approached from behind, peering up at it, hand cupped around his eyes against the setting sun. The leaves glittered and twisted in the breeze. He circled around it, slowly, becoming aware of shifting shapes and forms within the shimmering morass of leaves, nestled deep within the structure of the pillar.

As he came around the front of the grave, his eyes affixed to the bizarre sight before him, he finally realised what he was looking at. It was a sculpture: an image of a beautiful woman, shifting and turning with every eddy of the breeze, her hair fluttering loosely around her shoulders.

She turned, as if to look at him with her blank, shining eyes, and the expression on her face was immediately familiar. It was Charlotte Merrison.

Newbury staggered backwards, struck with a sudden sense of awe. He could see now that the leaves and stems incorporated exquisitely designed mechanisms, tiny cogs and wheels, levers and joints.

This had been Wither's final project – his last, magnificent piece of art. This is what he'd known as he committed himself to the flames – what Newbury had seen in his eyes as he'd died. All of it had been a performance. All of it had been leading to this. As Wither's body decomposed, it had sprouted, treated with whatever arcane or ingenious substances he had devised in the last months of his life. Somehow, he'd imagined *this*. He'd given his own life to once more give life, of a sort, to his lost love.

Newbury dropped to his knees. In no way did this wondrous piece of art absolve what Wither had done, the lives he had taken in pursuit of whatever demons had haunted his final days. But there was beauty in it, nonetheless.

He felt the prick of a tear in the corner of his eye. He wished Fred could have seen it. For months, the man had laboured to remove the strange growths, to honour the grave of an appalling killer – and in doing so he had held this beautiful, final act of love at bay.

Finally, Newbury understood. He saw what he and

Bainbridge had missed. Wither had taken his own life, and he had done so in pursuit of love and art. Out of all the death and horror, he had created something beautiful. He couldn't agree with what the man had done, but at least he now knew *why*.

Newbury got to his feet. He would send a note to Clifford Merrison. The man should see his sister one last time.

He started to walk away, then looked back, just as the breeze ruffled Charlotte's hair, and her face turned, captured for a moment as if she were looking back at him over her shoulder. He hoped that, wherever she was now, she had finally arrived at her castle on the moors.

George Mann is a *Sunday Times* bestselling novelist and scriptwriter. He's the author of the *Newbury & Hobbes* Victorian mystery series, as well as four novels about a 1920s vigilante known as The Ghost. He's also written bestselling *Doctor Who* novels, new adventures for Sherlock Holmes and the supernatural crime series, *Wychwood*.

His comic writing includes extensive work on *Doctor Who*, *Dark Souls*, *Warhammer 40,000* and a series based on *Newbury & Hobbes*, as well *Teenage Mutant Ninja Turtles* for younger readers. He's written audio scripts for *Doctor Who*, *Blake's 7*, *Sherlock Holmes*, *Warhammer 40,000* and more, and for a handful of high-profile mobile games. As Editor he's assembled four anthologies of original Sherlock Holmes fiction, as well as multiple volumes of *The Solaris Book of New Science Fiction* and *The Solaris Book of New Fantasy*.

His website is at www.george-mann.com.

Reckless Engineering

A Pax Britannia Story

Jonathan Green

~ July 1998 ~

I – One of Our Brains is Missing

Steam hissed from around the hatch as the seals disengaged and the circular stainless steel door swung open. The man from the ministry lowered his hand from the scanner, and the glowing green palm print quickly began to fade.

Inspector Allardyce of Scotland Yard took a step back as the clouds of condensing vapour enveloped him, filling his nostrils with an acrid aromatic soup of cryogenic coolants and formaldehyde. And then the mists parted and Allardyce found himself looking through the opening into the Vault itself; a great cylindrical shaft of gleaming, stainless steel, with a grilled metal walkway running around the top and an ornate cast iron handrail running around the top of that.

Allardyce turned his attention to the door. It had to be six feet thick if it was an inch, with great locking bars that, when engaged, projected into the cylindrical holes spaced equidistantly around the hatchway. The Inspector doubted that even a bomb detonated right on the threshold would be able to break it open.

The man from the ministry had entered a code on the keypad beside the door – having already done the same to gain access to the antechamber before the entrance to the Vault – and then had still been subjected to a palm-print and retinal scan before being able to open the door. Allardyce certainly couldn't have got in without him – Malahyde, that was the man's name – not without Malahyde being there.

Allardyce followed the man through the hatch onto the encircling platform. Opposite the entrance, the walkway projected slightly over the vertiginous drop below, the rail curving outwards to accommodate it. Rising from this projecting platform was a small cogitator terminal, set within the top of a teak-panelled plinth. It looked not unlike a plant stand missing its aspidistra.

"I must say, this is most irregular," Malahyde said, tapping a switch to awaken the cogitator.

"I'm sure it is," replied Allardyce, tentatively peering over the railing into the well-like stainless steel shaft. Below, robotic spiders scuttled over the gleaming vertical surface of the shaft, tending to those in their care in their own unknowable manner.

"I mean, this is a top secret facility."

"I'm sure it is," said the policeman. "I mean, what would the public say if they knew?"

The man from the ministry glared at him, some colour coming to his pinched cheeks at last.

The analytical engine clicked and chirruped and a monitor screen glowed into iridescent emerald life.

"So when exactly did you first notice that one of the inmates was missing?"

"We prefer to refer to them as guests," Malahyde said with quiet insistence.

"Yes, but the word 'guest' implies that they could leave

whenever they want, and nobody here's going anywhere, are they?"

"Hello, what's all this then?" came a voice from behind them that caused both the civil servant and the policeman to spin round in surprise. "Don't say you've started without me!"

"Quicksilver?" Allardyce exclaimed.

"Always so perceptive, Maurice," the new arrival replied, smiling wryly. He was wearing a plum crushed velvet jacket, plum corduroy trousers of a subtly different shade, and a white linen shirt, offset with diamond cufflinks that complimented the diamond tie-pin securing his canary yellow silk cravat, not to mention the diamond-headed cane held loosely in his left hand.

"That's Inspector to you," Allardyce railed. "I see you're back from wherever it is you've been this time."

"Like I say, perceptive as ever."

"The Moon, wasn't it?"

"In a roundabout sort of way."

"Nice eyepatch, by the way. You deserve each other."

"Excuse me, who is this man?" the man from the ministry, who went by the name of Malahyde, challenged. "And how did he get in here?"

"Ulysses Lucian Quicksilver at your service," the dandy replied, deftly flicking open a leather wallet and thrusting his crown-authorised credentials in the civil servant's face, "here to save the day."

"Does the day need saving?" Malahyde sniped.

"That's what we're here to find out, isn't it?" Quicksilver joined them inside the Vault as the spiders continued their strange nursemaid ballet. "I hear one of your brains has gone missing."

"We prefer to call them —"

"Guests," interrupted Allardyce. "They prefer to call them guests."

"That's as maybe," said Quicksilver, "but the term 'guest' suggests they're free to up sticks and leave whenever they want."

"I know, we've been through this already."

"So you *did* start without me." The dandy gave the policeman a petulant pout.

Allardyce's scowl deepened. "What are you doing here, anyway?"

"I received the same all channels alert I suspect you did," said Quicksilver.

"What?" exclaimed Malahyde.

Allardyce looked at him in bemusement. "Well if you didn't send the message, who did?"

The man from the ministry's fingers danced over the cogitator keyboard, accessing the Vault's data-log.

"It must have been an automatic signal sent out by the Vault itself," Malahyde said, sounding as if he could barely believe what he was suggesting.

"Reporting that one of its occupants had gone walkabout," Quicksilver said.

"Hardly!" snapped the man from the ministry. "Besides, until we entered the Vault five minutes ago, no one had entered or left the facility since the last regular maintenance check three days ago."

"Could it be a glitch in the system?" Quicksilver asked. "A ghost in the machine? Although, admittedly, that doesn't narrow it down much, because there are rather a lot of ghosts in this particular machine of yours, aren't there."

"It's possible," Malahyde admitted.

"Then I would suggest we start by checking to see if the errant 'guest' in question is actually missing," said Allardyce, feeling the need to wrest control of the situation from the interloper.

"Very well," said Malahyde, tapping a series of commands into the thinking machine.

A moment later, an articulated brass arm unfolded from the ceiling and a mechanical claw descended into the depths of the shaft. Somewhere, from far below, there was the distinct hiss of escaping gas, as a hermetic seal was broken and a sleek metal and glass tube slid out from the smooth wall of the shaft.

The claw grasped the tube and completed the job of extracting it from its surroundings. The arm retracted again, and the claw finally deposited the gleaming cylinder in a cradle that rose out of the platform in front of them to meet it.

It looked not unlike an oversized tablet capsule – a smooth cylinder with hemispherical ends, made completely from metal, apart from a glass panel halfway along its length. Through the glass, blurred by the viscous yellow-green liquid that filled the pod, could be seen the grey-pink flesh of a human brain, wires and electrodes connecting it to the containment unit.

Allardyce couldn't stop a gasp of amazement from escaping his slack-jawed mouth.

"So nothing has actually been stolen at all," Quicksilver said, matter-of-factly.

"So it would appear," admitted Malahyde, somewhat sheepishly.

"Are all your 'guests' kept like this?" Allardyce asked, staring in morbid fascination at the brain bobbing about in the preservative soup.

"Yes."

"So what exactly is this place?"

"Have you never heard of Think Tank, Maurice?" Quicksilver piped up. "You know how they say, all great minds think alike? Well they do here!"

"What do you mean?" Allardyce asked, flabbergasted.

"Think Tank is a secret Whitehall facility where the brains of supposedly dearly-departed geniuses are housed, so that they can keep working for the empire of Magna Britannia. I've heard rumours about this place for years. Only now I know they weren't rumours at all."

"The Vault it vital to the smooth running of empire!" the man from the ministry blustered. "How else do you think Magna Britannia has been able to keep leading the way in terms of technological developments? How do you think we, as a nation, have continued to make so many incredible scientific advances? If it weren't for this facility, Babbage would never have been able to perfect his analytical engine. And who do you think designed the second Crystal Palace?"

"Joseph Paxton?" hazarded Allardyce.

"Exactly."

"But I thought that the new construction was based on old designs of his."

"Then you thought wrong," said Quicksilver. "That's the trouble with the powers that be; they don't like letting go of the past. Just look at Her Majesty, if you're in any doubt."

"How many geniuses have you got stored here?" Allardyce asked.

The man from the ministry's answer, when it came, was lost beneath a cacophony of breaking class, rending metal, and the resounding crash of fifty-ton footsteps.

All eyes turned to the entrance to the Vault. A vast shadow fell across the atrium on the other side and then a massive mechanical hand reached through the open hatch.

The hand uncaringly knocked Allardyce aside, while Quicksilver deftly dodged out of the way.

The man from the ministry was not so fortunate. The huge robotic fist bludgeoned into him, pushing him over the railing and off the platform, his screams vanishing with him into the depths of the Vault.

It was quite clear, however, that the hand's intention had not been to remove any opposition, but simply to retrieve the metal pod containing the not-so-missing brain.

Cast iron fingers plucked the sealed cylinder from the metal claw and the hand retreated through the hatchway once more, with its prize firmly grasped.

Stumbling to his feet, Allardyce followed the hand through the hatch. Looking up through the shattered glass and steel roof of the atrium, he saw a looming figure silhouetted against the smoggy-orange morning sky, great clouds of steam puffing from what appeared to be a colossal stovepipe hat.

As he watched, dumbfounded, the towering automaton opened a door in its chest plate and placed the containment unit containing the brain inside, before slamming it shut again with a clang.

Gunfire echoed from outside, as the police fought to fend off the robotic invader.

"Who was it whose brain was supposed to have been stolen?" Allardyce shouted, suddenly finding his voice again.

The dandy detective scanned the cogitator's readout screen before turning and fixing Allardyce with his one remaining eye.

"Isambard Kingdom Brunel."

II – Brass Brunel

"So whose brain is it, sir?"

"Brunel's," Ulysses Quicksilver replied as his manservant, chauffeur and all-round bodyguard Nimrod steered the Mark IV Rolls Royce Silver Phantom through the busy London traffic; traffic that had been made even worse by the fact that a giant robot was at that moment crashing its uncaring way through the capital, heedless of the horse-drawn hansom cabs, chugging charabancs, steam-driven omnibuses and endless automobiles.

"So the original alert was just a ruse."

"Indeed. I would hazard that the esteemed engineer triggered the alert himself. Whatever else he might have been able to do from inside the Vault, he was locked out of tampering with the opening mechanism – a failsafe wisely put in by the Vault's original architects. And there was no way the robot could break in from the outside, either; the Vault's just too well-protected, too deeply-buried, and an open assault on the facility from outside would have led to an instant lockdown, leaving Brunel's brain trapped inside.

"He knew that if the Vault sent a message saying that one of the brains had been stolen someone would be forced to investigate. When Inspector Allardyce suggested we extract the containment unit to check that the brain *was* actually missing, it was as if he had gift-wrapped it for Brunel. With the Vault open, he merely had to send his robot familiar in to finish the job."

Ahead of them, further along Edgware Road, the colossal automaton continued on its way, paying no heed to the panicking people and chaotic traffic beneath feet, as drivers attempted to slew their vehicles out of the way of its car-crushing footfalls.

"Ah, yes, the robot, sir," said Nimrod, pulling hard on the steering wheel and swinging the automobile right to avoid a charging hansom cab, the horse pulling it fleeing in panic, foam flying from the corners of its mouth. "How was the esteemed engineer – or what was left of him – able to have this monstrosity ready and waiting for him when he did eventually effect his own release?"

"I can only surmise that this has been a plan long in the making and that Brunel hid the designs for his cast iron saviour among the plans for something else. As many factories are now fully automated anyway, no one would have realised that among the Think Tank's designs was one for a colossal robot."

"So, robots building robots. Well, that's just a ridiculous notion," muttered Nimrod.

"It is the future," Ulysses countered.

"And is there still a place for human servants in this future of yours, sir? Maybe those neo-Luddites – those so-called 'Steam Punks' – have a point."

"Now-now, old chap, don't be like that. You're irreplaceable."

"Nonetheless, you would think someone would have noticed a giant robot making its way through London, right to the seat of government in Whitehall."

"Hmm," mused Ulysses. "Good point. You didn't see anything, I suppose?"

"Not until it was too late and the machine was right on top of you."

Ahead of them, further along the Edgware Road, the colossal automaton reached up with one iron arm, grabbed hold of the metalwork of one of the lower stretches of the London Overground and pulled. Accompanied by a sound that resembled a hundred head-on collisions, a fifty-yard stretch of the suspended railway came crashing down into the street, crushing automobiles and delivery vans beneath it and creating an instant barricade to stop anyone attempting to follow.

"Curses!" Quicksilver exclaimed as Nimrod brought the Phantom to a screeching halt, parallel to the makeshift barrier.

Hastily taking out his personal communicator, he keyed in a number using the enamel keypad set within the brass and teak body of the device.

"Inspector?" he spoke into the handset. "Was in pursuit but have just met with a slight setback. Any ideas where the robot's taking Brunel?"

There was a moment's buzz of static interference from the other end of the line before Allardyce answered. "Eyes in the sky say it looks to be heading towards Paddington Station."

"That would make sense," Ulysses replied, and then to Nimrod: "Paddington Station, and don't spare the horses!"

"Perish the thought, sir," Nimrod replied. Putting the car into gear and revving the engine, he took off again through the confused chaos that was typical of the streets of Londinium Maximum, especially when there was a giant robot loose in the city.

"Shall we meet you there?" Ulysses asked into the mouthpiece of his communicator.

His question was met by a string of expletives from the other end and a noise that sounded very much like a devastating car crash.

"Allardyce? Are you still there? Are you alright?"

"Looks as if you're on your own!" came the Inspector's

agitated voice.

"Why? What's happened?"

"It's our cars! Our own cars! They –" Abruptly, the line went dead.

"Sir, is everything alright?" Nimrod asked, swinging the car left and driving it at full throttle the wrong way up a one-way street.

"No, it's not," Ulysses replied. "In fact I think everything is very un-alright."

III – GWR

A matter of minutes later, a Rolls Royce Silver Phantom turned onto the entrance ramp that led down to Paddington Station. Barely slowing at all, it bumped over the gated barrier that had been flattened beneath a giant steel foot and drove into the station forecourt.

Nimrod didn't need to ask for directions to determine which way to go; the trail of devastation ahead of them told them all they needed to know. Besides, it would have been hard to miss the colossus as it strode across the concourse, its stove-pipe chimney-hat scraping the roof struts supporting the famed glazed roof – one of Brunel's own designs – even as it ducked to make its way through the station. Only, Ulysses realised, the robot wasn't crouching down, it was transforming.

As Nimrod steered the Silver Phantom along the platform, its Rolls Royce engine roaring and people screaming as they threw themselves out of the way of the speeding vehicle, the huge automaton's legs folded beneath it. Great iron wheels emerged as panels opened in its cast iron calves, while its haunches took on the appearance of an engineman's cab.

The robot's arms opened, revealing more wheels, while what Ulysses had at first taken to be the joints of the mechanical's elbows were also revealed to be spoked iron wheels. Its cylindrical body, which contained the boiler and the source of its motive power, became the boiler-body of the engine, while its neck ratchetted backwards so that its head, with those crude man-like features, became the front of the locomotive, its stove-pipe hat forming the chimney.

With its wheels engaged on the track, steam hissing from piston-joints and smoke puffing from its chimney, the scowling engine began to move, quickly picking up speed.

"Well at least we now know how the robot managed to sneak up on everyone in Whitehall," said Ulysses. "It was hiding in plain sight, probably at the Westminster Overground Station, and then transformed and climbed down from the Circle Line when Brunel's brain signalled that the Vault had been opened."

"Quite, sir," acknowledged Nimrod.

The Silver Phantom continued to race along the platform, hurtling towards the barrier at its end, where the brickwork of the platform descended abruptly and became subsumed by the gravel, rails and sleepers of the railway as the multiple tracks emerged from the station.

For a moment, Ulysses considered flinging open the car door, balancing himself on the sill and then throwing himself at the altered automaton before it could escape. But, apart from the obvious risk to his own life, were he to try such a thing, what would he be able to achieve once he was on board? As far as he was aware, the newly-transformed locomotive didn't come with controls for a driver, and what was to say it wouldn't simply turn back into a robot and grind him into the track beneath its feet?

As the car accelerated towards the end of the platform, Ulysses wondered whether Nimrod was planning on somehow using a conveniently placed porter's cart as a ramp to leap the Phantom onto the roof of the puffing locomotive. But then, with the cast iron barrier only a matter of yards away and with a snarl of annoyance, Nimrod slammed on the brakes. Accompanied by the smell of burning rubber, the automobile slewed to a halt, Nimrod thumping his hands down on the steering wheel in frustration.

Ulysses could do nothing but watch as the train-cum-automaton chugged out of the station and away down the line.

"Time for Plan B, I feel," said Ulysses. "Back up, would you, old chap?"

"Of course, sir," his faithful manservant replied, his more characteristic calm and unflappable veneer restored. Putting the car into reverse, Nimrod backed the vehicle along the platform.

Upon reaching what was left of the passenger turnstiles at the concourse end of the platform – that had also been flattened during the automaton's rampage – Nimrod brought the car to a halt as an overweight individual in the uniform of a station manager puffed over to them.

Winding down the window, Ulysses poked his head out and asked, "Where does that line go to, my good man?"

"That's the GWR line," the fat controller replied. "Looks like your Great Western Robot's on its way to Bristol."

"Then Bristol it is, Nimrod," Ulysses said, tapping the back of the leather-upholstered driver's seat with his diamond-tipped cane.

IV – Shipshape and Bristol Fashion

The sun was setting over Bristol Harbour as the locomotive pulled into the dockyard, a ball of molten iron in a liquid gold sky painting the masts of the recently restored SS Great Britain crimson. The engine came to a stop with a great hiss of steam, as if relaxing its piston-muscles after its long run from the capital to the West Country. But then almost instantly, with another great exhalation of steam – the water vapour clouding in the evening air – the machine transformed once more.

Its iron chassis unfolding, the engine's boiler becoming the trunk of its automaton body, the cab becoming legs again, and its truck wheels and piston rods folding back into its arms as it took on the form of a giant iron man once more, stove-pipe hat firmly in place upon its great cast iron head.

The automaton's great head turned from left to right and back again, its machine senses scanning the barn-like industrial sheds, the dry docks and the construction yards, as if this brass Brunel was furtively checking to make sure that no one had been watching from the shadows as it changed. But the docks were quiet. The day shift had ended long ago and everyone had gone home for the night.

Moving as stealthily as a hundred-ton robot could, the iron giant made its way towards one of the colossal warehouse-like edifices. But before it could reach the great iron doors of the shed, it was caught in the wide beams of a barrage of blazing lights.

The robot came to an abrupt halt mid-stride. The lights were positioned atop two towering cranes that stood at the harbour-side.

As the automaton stood frozen, its mechanical mind reassessing the situation, the jibs of the cranes spun round, dragging the heavy, cast-iron hooks suspended at the end of their cable hoists through the air, swinging them towards the automaton like twin wrecking balls.

One of the hooks clanged into the cylindrical body of the robot, the booming echo of the contact resounding over the dockyards. The huge automaton stumbled, catching the hook suspended from the other derrick as it turned to face its attackers.

Grasping the hook in its huge hands, the robot sent it swinging back towards the crane gantry. The jib was pulled round, momentum swinging it away from the robot. But the first crane swung its hook again, hitting the robot from behind this time.

The brass Brunel stumbled again, but remained on its feet. And then the robot was on the move once more, but so were the cranes.

As the colossal automaton clumped towards the construction

shed, the four gantry legs that supported the engine-house of each lifting engine disengaged from their dockside moorings and the two cranes galloped across the gravel surface of dockyard after the fleeing droid.

"What's the plan, sir?" Nimrod's voice crackled over the radio that connected the two cranes, so that those operating the machines could do so in perfect unison. Could Ulysses detect a suggestion of excitement in his manservant's usual monotone drawl? "Knock the robot's block off and once it's out for the count recover Brunel's brain?"

Ulysses pulled back on the drive lever and pushed down hard on the power pedal, putting the crane he was piloting into reverse as the Brunel-automaton suddenly turned. The heavy links of a chain in its vice-like hands, it swung the solid iron anchor attached to the end in Ulysses' direction. One prong of the anchor clipped the side of the cab, tearing a hole in the hut-like construction and sending splintered planks and twisted spars of metal flying across the yard.

"Let's just worry about knocking it down first, shall we?" came Ulysses' breathless reply.

Ulysses battled to put the crane into a forward gear again. "Come on, you stubborn bastard!" he bellowed. And then, the gearbox stopped fighting and he found the gear he was looking for. Sooty black clouds puffing from its smokestack, Ulysses drove Lifting Engine No. 2 – also known as 'Cranky' to the men who worked the docks day in, day out – towards the automaton, before the robot could swing its lethal weapon again or try to turn tail and flee into the construction sheds.

Pulling on another lever, he spun the engine cab about, the crane's long boom rotating with it, smashing into the robot once again. Nimrod had managed to steer his crane, Lifting Engine No. 1 – known as 'Steeve' to the yard's work crews – round behind the brass Brunel so that his derrick now stood between the automaton and the corrugated iron barn.

The mobile gantry appeared – to Ulysses, at least – to hunker down, as if bracing itself, assuming a fighter's stance. An articulated grappling claw that formed its secondary limb constricted, bunching into a fist, and then abruptly powered forward like a boxer. As the automaton tried to find its footing after the blow it had received from the boom of Lifting Engine No. 2, Engine No. 1 sent it reeling back the other way with a resounding blow to the head.

Under the force of the blow, the brass Brunel's neck joint snapped with a sharp crack. The cast iron head lolled sideways at an unnatural angle, even for a transforming robot. The mechanical giant stumbled, a foot passing over the edge of one of the shipyard's dry docks, and with a series of echoing clangs it tumbled into the waterless void. It collided with the SS Great Britain, currently occupying the dock while it underwent extensive restoration work, leaving the ship rocking on its wooden stays.

Ulysses peered out through the grime-smeared cab windows, trying to see what had happened to the robot. Was it down? Had they truly defeated it at last? Perhaps if he could just get a little closer...

For a moment he considered climbing down from the crane to take a look but then thought better of it. Putting the drive lever into first gear and applying gentle pressure to the power pedal, he walked Lifting Engine No. 2 towards the black void of the dry dock. Nimrod did the same with Lifting Engine No. 1.

As the two cranes reached the edge of the pit, a large mechanical hand formed of gleaming brass pistons and sheet steel reached out of the blackness and clamped shut around one of the gantry legs of Nimrod's machine. Even as Ulysses' manservant tried to pull back, the brass Brunel pulled harder. With one leg no longer in contact with the ground, the remaining three splayed feet of the crane slid through the gravel and oil-soaked black earth of the yard, gouging great ruts in the filthy ground in the process.

Still holding the crane's leg in its left hand, the automaton rose from the pit once more, its head still cantilevered strangely to the right, and swung its right hand – now bunched into a fist – at another of the lifting engine's legs. The girder struts of the leg buckled under the force of the blow and suddenly Nimrod found his machine tipping forwards, unbalanced. Crane-arm and claw-limb flailing, there was nothing he could do to halt the derrick's inexorable fall as the crane crashed to the ground, coming to rest with the driver's cab protruding over the end of the dry dock. Window panes shattered under the impact, as the brass Brunel hauled itself out of the pit.

"I'm down, sir," came Nimrod's frustrated voice. "It's floored me."

"Have no fear!" Ulysses declared, putting Lifting Engine No. 2 into gear and driving its accelerator pedal to the floor. "Ulysses Quicksilver is here!"

The gantry galloped across the dockyard like some crazed giraffe. As it powered forward, rather than swing the jib of the crane at the automaton again, Ulysses lowered the boom so that the metalwork of the crane became a lance of reinforced steel, aimed directly at the robot's boiler body.

The crane speared the iron giant, buckling under the impact, as did the cylindrical body of the robot. High pressure super-heated steam escaped from the split Cranky had ripped in the boiler sleeve and for a moment Ulysses thought he saw something like startled surprise in the headlamp eyes of the robot's lolling head. In that moment he understood what was about to happen and threw himself to the floor of the cab as the boiler body of the brass Brunel exploded.

Every window of Lifting Engine No. 2 shattered, diamond shards raining down around Ulysses as well as on top of him, while a spear of twisted, scalding metal thudded into the wooden planks that formed the back wall of the cab and stayed there.

The boom of the catastrophic explosion still echoing around the warehouses and storage sheds, Ulysses cautiously picked himself up. As he peered out of the glass-less windows of the driver's cab, into the deepening gloom, he could hear what sounded like the patter of rainfall, but he could not see any rain spots turning the grey gravel black. It took him a moment to realise that it wasn't rain but the sound of tiny pieces of debris from the destruction of the automaton landing out in the harbour.

There was nothing left intact of the robot's boiler body and Ulysses couldn't see anything of its head either. He wouldn't be surprised if, even now, the head was sinking into the water's dark depths. What was left of the droid's legs lay on the ground at the harbour's edge.

Ulysses clambered down from the cab and joined Nimrod where he stood beside the ruined remains of the robot, his manservant having also climbed free of his fallen lifting engine.

"The bigger they are," the older man remarked as they surveyed the shattered inner workings of the brass Brunel, the hot metal plinking as it began to cool.

"And they don't get much bigger than Isambard Kingdom Brunel," Ulysses replied. "But it looks as if his days of reckless engineering are over for good."

"You don't think his brain could have survived the destruction of the droid?" Nimrod hazarded.

"I suppose it's possible that the containment unit protected it from the worst of the damage," Ulysses pondered, "and splashed down in the river. But if that's the case it would take a very concerted effort to find and retrieve it. I think it just as likely that the pod was ripped apart by the explosion too, and that his brain was flash-fried the instant the boiler blew."

The two men peered at the settling black mirror of the harbour waters, lost in thought as each contemplated the fate of the greatest engineering mind Magna Britannia had ever known.

"But it's for the authorities to decide whether they want to even attempt to find any evidence of Brunel's demise amongst the wreckage here. And if they do, I'm sure when they're done sifting the debris they'll leave everything shipshape and Bristol fashion."

"Talking of the authorities, sir," Nimrod said.

"You think I should let Allardyce know what has happened to his missing brain? If I can get hold of him, that is."

"You know what he's like, sir."

"Yes, and for that very reason, the good inspector can wait," Ulysses said. "Besides, I'd rather deliver the bad news face to face, assuming he still has a face I can deliver to, if it's all the same to you, old chap."

V – Errors of Today

"Dead?!?"

"I assume so," Ulysses Quicksilver said, "considering the mess made by the exploding robot."

Inspector Maurice Allardyce winced, clearly dreading what sort of trouble he was going to get in with his bosses at Scotland Yard for not only losing Brunel's brain on his watch but then failing to recover it.

It had been bad enough that the Met's own vehicles had turned on them at the crucial moment, transforming into something akin to armoured knights. It turned out that they had been designed by the un-deceased Brunel as well; four officers had lost their lives, and another twelve had been seriously injured, before they were able to put them down. After that debacle, he had been pinning his hopes on Quicksilver bringing him some good news, not that he would ever admit that to the arrogant toff himself.

"I thought you said you were going to sort this mess out," Allardyce challenged the dandy.

"We brought the guilty party to justice, didn't we?"

"If by 'guilty party' you mean Isambard Kingdom Brunel, then yes, it would appear you well and truly stopped him, more's the pity."

"You didn't tell me you were expecting us to recover his brain," Quicksilver pointed out coldly.

"I would have thought that went without saying," Allardyce snapped.

"Besides, it might still be lying at the bottom of the River Avon somewhere, although by now I expect it will have travelled some distance downstream."

"I believe the search has already begun. The local constabulary seemed very eager. Something about Brunel being an adopted Bristol boy."

"Well there you go then. All's well that ends well, as they say."

"But this hasn't ended well." The inspector's shoulders slumped dejectedly.

"I think we're done here just the same, don't you?" Quicksilver turned, starting for the door.

"There is one thing I've been meaning to ask you," Allardyce said, as the dandy took hold of the door handle.

Quicksilver turned again and fixed Allardyce with his one remaining eye. "And what would that be, Maurice?"

"How did you beat the robot down to Bristol?"

"Well, for one thing I'll have you know that Nimrod and I held the record for the Paris-Dakar rally between us for eight years running. But aside from that, you know what the rail network is like. Delays at Didcot, a points failure at Slough, the wrong kind of leaves on the line – there's always something."

VI – Kingdom

Isambard Kingdom Brunel stood at the arching apex of the Ironbridge and gazed across the acres of manufactory spread out before him, resembling some vast industrial metropolis, as clouds of smog drifted by high overhead. The sides of the gorge were still there, only now they were adorned with a tangle of pipework that covered the cliffs like a pernicious growth of iron ivy.

This was the place where the Industrial Revolution had begun, more than a century and a half before. The Ironbridge Gorge had been roofed over long ago, the village and some ten thousand acres becoming subsumed into one vast factory complex, along with Coalbrookdale and Jackfield as well, where automated production lines worked ceaselessly, day and night, to forge the machines that kept the British empire of Magna Britannia in operation.

The River Severn no longer passed under the bridge itself, having long ago been diverted to satisfy the water requirements of the industrial plant. Brick and tile works, blast furnaces and coal, iron and fire clay mines all existed now within the confines of the factory itself. The place even had its own network of canals.

A visitor to the region in the eighteenth century – upon witnessing Coalbrookdale by night, the settlement seeming as bright as day, with its endless clouds of smoke under-lit by the fires of the incessant foundries – had described the Gorge as being akin to a vision of Hell. Well, that description was only all the more apt now. And the factory was as hot as Hades as well, not that such things as temperature and atmospheric pollution mattered to Brunel.

An ordinary man would have found it hard to even catch his breath in this place, but Brunel was no ordinary man, and never had been.

He drummed clockwork fingers on the rail of the bridge as he surveyed his army spread out below, his great work come to fruition at last. His new body suited him much better. It was on an altogether more human scale and its workings were the most intricate he had ever devised.

It had been a simple thing for a mind such as Brunel's – used to planning things with the minutest precision, down to the smallest detail – to evade the authorities, swapping places with the other automaton-engine at Swindon. While his replacement had continued to lead his pursuers a merry dance all the way down to Bristol docks, he had transferred onto the Cheltenham line, and from there made his way, via Birmingham, to Shropshire and the Iron Gorge industrial complex.

He took in the ranks of giant automata, his Brass Brunels, their stovepipe chimney-hats puffing steam into the smoke-fogged atmosphere that reeked of coal-tar, row after row of the colossal robots, made in his own image, filling the factory floor.

This place was where the Industrial Revolution had begun before and here was where it would begin anew.

Magna Britannia would pay for what had been done to him and all those countless other great minds imprisoned within the Vault.

It was time for the machines to arise. It was time for a new age of steam. It was time for a new Industrial Revolution.

Jonathan Green is a writer of speculative fiction, with more than seventy books to his name. He has written everything from *Fighting Fantasy* gamebooks to *Doctor Who* novels, by way of *Sonic the Hedgehog*, *Teenage Mutant Ninja Turtles*, *Judge Dredd*, *Robin of Sherwood*, and *Frostgrave*. He is the creator of the *Pax Britannia* steampunk series for Abaddon Books, and has written eight novels and numerous short stories set within this steampunk universe, featuring the debonair dandy adventurer Ulysses Quicksilver. He is the author of the award-winning, and critically-acclaimed, *YOU ARE THE HERO – A History of Fighting Fantasy Gamebooks*. He also edits and compiles short story anthologies. You can follow him on Twitter @jonathangreen and find out more about his current projects at: www.JonathanGreenAuthor.com.

The Athenian Dinner Party

Derry O'Dowd

The butterfly escaped the attentions of the young white cat by hovering above him, before landing on the stone sill of the house at 52 Queen Street, Edinburgh.

She wore her colours proudly; they mirrored the setting of the sun that could just be discerned behind the castle on the hill: umber, burnt orange, gold and sepia. The butterfly spread her wings and settled by the sash window, which was opened a little to admit the pleasant September evening breeze that recalled summer in its memories.

Inside the window and through the open curtains was a pleasant Victorian dining-room, high of ceiling, with a decorative rose in its centre from which hung a gas lamp chandelier of bronze with glass cups open as flowers to the sun. An ornately scrolled mirror graced the darkly papered wall above the mantel, where a clock ticked away the sands of time. To the sides were plates of finest bone, decorated in the Chinoiserie style, and a small Turkish rug of bright origins lay before the gently heating fire to catch any tiny embers. Beneath this, another larger rug, softer on the eye, traversed the length and width of the room, covering the deeply patinated wooden floorboards. Bookcases wilted under tomes of medicine and the assorted classics.

A gleaming mahogany table sat proudly in the centre of the room surrounded by button back chairs, including a carver at the head. A screen stood to one side of the table, a credenza to the other; the curios that sat atop its gleaming surface gave a truth which proclaimed that the gentleman who owned this house was rather out of the ordinary.

Some Hae Meat

'"Some hae meat and canna eat, and some wad eat that want it, but we hae meat and we can eat, and sae the Lord be thankit",' declared James Young Simpson in avuncular fashion, running his finger along his clean-shaven upper lip, then through his luxuriant under-chin beard before reaching for his cutlery.

'He admires Robbie Burns so,' declared his wife Jessie, her beautiful face softened to pretty through the years of childbearing, hair bound up to either side of her head and loosely pinned. An intricate brooch of jet adorned her dress at the breastbone.

'Oh Jessie so fair, I do love you so, could you think to fancy me?' responded her husband playfully, placing his hand on the lace cuff of her sleeve.

Marion Sims sat in peaceful reflection before the food, observing the amusing behaviour of the Scottish folk, a small smile tugging the corners of lips as he reached for his silver service.

'Aye, Marion, welcome once again to our home here in Edinburgh, the Athens of the North, named for our great castle on the hill yonder, and our love of Greek literature.' Simpson gesticulated towards their guest. 'And this room, nay our Letheon grotto, dedicated to Hypnos and his wing'd son Morpheus, the God of dreams, who enters through gates of ivory and horn.'

'But now Marion "Ye Pow'rs wha mak mankind your care, dish them out their bill o' fare" your vittels, should I say ambrosia, await.'

The Celestial Liquid of the Age

After the meal was cleared, Simpson ambled to the credenza to acquire a treasured memento. Placing the maroon coloured leather container in the centre of the table, he removed a bottle of clear liquid from its safe-keeping within.

'It was in this very grotto that it all began,' he remarked, holding the bottle to the light. 'Chloroform, this sweet smelling fluid.'

'We sat around our dining room table with my sister and Captain Petrie the night we first sampled its glory,' confirmed Jessie, smoothing her silken skirts.

'My parents, and me,' Agnes declared emphatically.

'And my colleagues Keith and Duncan,' continued Simpson. 'Eventually the chloroform anaesthetic was blessed by Queen Victoria herself, her pangs of childbirth defeated. The women of the nation followed suit. 'More chloroform!' they cried in exultation.'

'The vapour from the chloroform was so powerful,' said Jessie, recalling the experiment.

'The first inhalation brought excitement and great mental clarity. We told fantastic tales and thought new scientific methods.' Simpson nodded his leonine head.

'But I became an angel with poetic zephyrs that transported me,' Agnes said with wonder, laughing.

'One inhalation led to another, then near disaster, Ring a Ring o' Roses, and all fell under the mahogany,' sighed Jessie.

'We had discovered the celestial fluid chloroform, anaesthetic of the age.' Simpson's voice was quiet, considered.

Marion Sims observed intently as the slight, softly spoken man with Carolina in his cadence recited from memory, "The man who emerges with fame, whose mind gropes for lofty ideals, to bring them to light, must first with rigid frugality study his part".'

'Aha! We have a scholar in our midst.' Simpson paused, in reflection. 'An icon of Satyrs perhaps?' he remarked with some relish. 'But enough of classics, what say you we open our minds?' and as he looked around the table, his wife caught his eye.

'No more than five drops of the celestial liquid only, for fear of drowsiness on the floor,' she said.

'I could dream on a magic carpet,' Agnes wiggled her toes in her soft slippers.

'Come now Marion, we all espouse the Presbyterian ethic.

There is no harm in experimenting with chemicals to seek better physic for our kin-folk,' Simpson jollied his visitor along. 'But first, let us make a list of problems to solve before our minds begin a-wandering.'

In a moment, Jessie declared 'My, oh my! Just one item penned here for enlightenment but perhaps not suitable for delicate ears,' she cast a glance in the direction of her niece.

'"When even children lisp the Rights of Man; amid this mighty fuss just let me mention..."' quoted Simpson to his wife.

'Aye indeed,' she acknowledged with a nod.

'The rights of Woman merit some attention,' husband and wife recited together.

'Thank you, my love,' said Simpson as Agnes carried a plaster bust to the table from the credenza.

'This effigy is a copy of is the first child born under anaesthesia.' The dining guests regarded the baby's cherub lips, eyes closed as if asleep. 'The poor woman could not deliver as her pelvis was merely one half the expected size. Her first infant was stillborn and delivered piecemeal. With her second pregnancy, she was in obstructed labour with no chance of birthing. The Fates hovered round her life's thread. I administered the anaesthetic, turned the child, and with excessive struggle extracted the wee bairn feet first,' he spoke softly, sadly.

Marion lifted the likeness of the tiny child, noting the substantial concavity on the right side of the baby's skull. 'A large indent, pressure on the brain from the narrowed birth channel, fatal. A pitiful outcome,' he paused. 'Yes, there is but one item to discuss. The jeopardies of difficult childbirth.' Sims ran his fingers gently over the baby's face and returned the bust to the table.

Gyrus and Sulcus

Removing the top from the chloroform bottle, Simpson placed a few drops on proffered linen handkerchiefs, and re-stoppered the vial.

Soon after inhalation. Marion sang in a pleasant tone, 'The wavy ringlets of her flaxen hair, floating in the summer air, the gentle power of Rosalie the Desert Flower.'

'Luve's like a Red, Red Rose that's newly sprung,' trilled Simpson over the Southern gentleman's vocals.

'Hush, and let ye be talking childbirth,' chuckled Jessie in a mock-strong accent.

'Sufficient to frighten your loving niece,' giggled Agnes.

The moment passed, elation abounded, and each gyrus and sulcus sparkled in the bilateral hemispheres of Scottish and American brains.

Automatic Continuous Body Closure

Simpson trod the room heavily, hands behind his back. Marion stood by the window observing the street scene, passers-by enjoying the evening air before night drew her cloak tightly to display the stellar firmament. A cabby closed his coat against the coolness now apparent, and the butterfly, tired of her sill, flitted into the room.

'Caesareans are dangerous, but your "wee bairn" would have survived the operation. Being Professor of Midwifery you may not favour that surgery.' Marion turned from the street view to the room.

'Less than one in five mothers survive. Tissue destruction, blood loss, putrefaction of the wound.' Simpson's pacing stopped and he faced Marion. 'But you are aware from your American practice of the perils of caesareans, even in this year of Our Lord 1861.'

'Indeed… I observed a man close his coat there on the street,' Marion mused as he took his seat. 'Could we treat the lower belly akin to a coat and devise an open then close method. Lift the baby out of the matrix and close all up again safely, with no fear of copious blood loss?'

Jessie began to speak, hesitated, and then uttered with conviction, 'James, 'twas in the Scotsman.'

'Out with it Jessie, I am lost,' replied her husband, who trod a track through the convolutions of the Turkish rug.

'In America. I kept the news cutting in my sewing box. A man invented an Automatic Continuous Clothing Closure, pulled together with a string.' Jessie spoke the words over her shoulder as she went to retrieve the article.

'His name was Elias Howe,' she read on her return.

'Howe? How, what, when, where, why, in what way, by what means?' mused Marion.

'Ah the quis, quid, quando etcetera of Hermagoras,' muttered Simpson.

'So, when suturing the wounds of the first Caesarean, fit an Automatic Continuous Body Closure. Pull a clasp or string to "Open Sesame" when the next childbirth is imminent.' Marion looked to his own belly to demonstrate. 'Remove the bairn from its cosy nest in the womb. After the birth, close the womb and other structures by a simple tug on the clasp.'

'The man in the moon and his wife would be so happy,' Agnes said, smiling.

The Osseus Porta

'You are asthenic are you not, Marion?' asked Simpson. 'While I am somewhat less so.'

'Yes, and we both inhaled the same quantity. In truth, another dose of chloroform is required for you, kind sir. I prescribe it thus,' Marion beamed.

While Simpson availed of the opportunity to inhale more vapour, Marion spoke with Jessie. 'I cannot help but observe that stone with pins adherent.' He gestured towards the sewing box.

Agnes intervened, 'Uncle James collects rocks.' Her cheeks flushed as becomingly pink as her gown.

'An interest in geology and archaeology, he tells me,' Jessie tutted. 'The house is burdened, and books of all sorts.'

'Lapis magnes, the Magnesian stone. It is a lodestone, Marion, I presume your awareness. The attractive facility for iron within the nugget was discovered by the ancient Greek tribe that inhabited Magnesia.' Simpson halted at the burgeoning bookcase to retrieve a favourite tome on that civilisation.

'What if...' Marion spoke, paused, fingers dancing across the table top. 'But would it work? For the women of low stature or whose pelvis is as small as you described?' He closed his fists then brought them close together, knuckles almost touching.

'This is perhaps an American riddle you task us with?' Simpson looked up from the book which he held in his hands.

'Oh Uncle, do cease and desist,' Agnes chided him affectionately as only those who hold a close kinship can.

'The bones of the pelvic girdle almost touch at the front but there is a slim cushion of tissue between, the symphysis pubis.' Marion took his kerchief and inserted it between his closed fists. 'Like so. Why not incise the slim cushion during the first caesarean. Insert lodestone and a ferrous object and attach to either bony end. The pelvic girdle would be locked in a magnetic embrace. Undo that encirclement to open the pelvis. The infant would escape more easily.' He moved his fists apart.

'But what is the key to unlock the embrace?' asked Jessie.

'Your attention, one moment, may I be so bold as to utter words of wisdom?' Simpson opened the book in his hands. 'The Greek tribe of Magnetes discovered the loadstone. And here,' he pointed to the tome, 'it is written further in Hesiod's poem The Catalogue of Women, "The sweet-voiced Olympia Muses, they who were the best in those days, loosed their girdles to give birth". Could it be that those heroic women of ancient Greece opened their pelvic girdles for childbirth? In days so far away?'

'The key, Jessie, there is your answer,' said Marion, inspired, excited. 'Far away, Faraday, Michael Faraday. He electrified magnets to increase their power. Apply in this instance and a rock-solid pelvic girdle would result. Undo that electro-magnetic attraction with a retro-current when required. Voilà, a pelvis unlocked, the infant escapes. Electrify the Magnesian stones once more until the next birth.'

The Dark Olympian

The gas lights hissed above their heads and Jessie rested her chin on her hand as the American guest wove his story.

'The poor girl was incurable. Her fate was to live as an outcast, abandoned by the father of her stillborn child, unable to continue as a servant in the plantation house, living on scraps. A consequence of her difficult childbirth.'

'A most cruel fate,' Jessie said, greatly saddened.

'Her urine flowed day and night, the bedding and clothing saturated. The delicate skin of the female parts and thighs was inflamed. Ulcers and blisters were a torment that caused unremitting pain and burning akin to smallpox. The malodour permeated every corner of her room so that her life was one of suffering and disgust.'

'Death would have been preferable,' remarked Agnes, troubled.

'But patients of this kind never die, they must live and suffer.' Simpson covered his niece's hand with his own.

'Untoward and prolonged pressure on the bladder base during a difficult slow birth led to a mortification. The tissue sloughed and an opening between bladder and birth canal larger than a silver dollar allowed urine to escape unfettered. Anarcha was just a teenager. Many more women in America, here in Europe, Africa and Asia are similarly affected.' Marion trailed his napkin through his fingers.

'But you are rightly famed as the surgeon who first cured women of those fistulae,' said Simpson, 'for which you founded the world's first hospital for women in New York.'

'A time for healing of the affected tissues before surgery would benefit.' Marion's statement posed a query.

The fire consumed the wood, a cool breeze ruffled the curtain as Jessie slid the sash window shut and turned to speak.

'The wives of Edinburgh make elbow patches for worn out coats. Would a temporary patch in the birth canal suffice?'

'Indeed, a flap of skin interposed as postulated by Jobert,

Velpeau and Leroy.' Simpson faced his wife. 'But the notion is without success to date.'

'Perhaps the Olympic Muses in whom you delight may yield a reaction,' spoke Agnes.

Simpson gazed at the titles as he rummaged through of his beloved books. 'You, Agnes, are a wonder. So, Jessie, the books that burden our home reveal their beauty.' Triumphantly, he read, "Galen, de Compositione Pharma-corum book four, 531. Fuscum Olympoinico inscriptum, the Dark Olympic Victor's Ointment".'

Walking back to the table, he offered the book. 'Marion, for you.'

'Facit ad maximos Dolores, for severe pain,' Marion read and translated.

'Explain further,' Simpson urged his guest.

'The ingredients of the ointment are: "Cadmia burnt and washed eight drachma", with acacia, antimony, aloes, crocus, myrrh, opium, gum, water and an egg. Make a thick paste. Add pomphylox and frankincense,' recited Marion.

'All the materials are available in our Edinburgh Dispensatory. This paste laid on skin would hold fast and becomes solid,' Simpson declared.

'Could it be the elbow patch Marion requires to stem the flow of urine?' Jessie mused.

'Add extra gum to render the patch ever more adhesive?' enquired Agnes.

'Cleanse and dry the sodden area in the birth channel. Apply the Dark Olympic Victor's Ointment with extra gum, allow to dry and become adherent. The channel is closed temporarily so the urine escapes as normal through the designated passageway. The tender skin heals. Then, surgery. We may have found a solution.' Marion was almost beyond jubilation.

'Appraise the outcome to the Dark Olympic patch, repeat as required. A sympatexic, excuse me, the celestial water is at fault, a sympathetic outcome.' Simpson grinned.

Jessie placed the stoppered chloroform into its case. 'We should partake of some Saloop now for 'tis nearly time for sweet departures.'

'"We four have paddled in the stream, from morning sun till dine, but seas between us broad have roared, since days of long ago",' Marion launched into a Scottish accent. 'My Teresa reads Robbie to our children at night.' He smiled innocently at Simpson, Jessie and Agnes.

The roar of laughter from Simpson was infectious, and none of them noticed at first when a butterfly the hues of sunset landed on his sleeve. As she flapped her wings, a flash of colour caught his eye and he looked down.

'My! What a beautiful creature you are,' he said, delighted at her presence.

'Hamearis Lucina I believe. Named for Lucina the Goddess of Childbirth,' declared Marion.

The butterfly fluttered above the mahogany table, an altar to the Oracle of Delphi, and gossamer wings conveyed the message: where knowledge blooms, then will arise belief, hope and redemption for the rights of women and all of mankind.

James Young Simpson, a prominent Scottish obstetrician, introduced anaesthesia to childbirth, while J. Marion Sims is the father of modern gynaecology. Simpson would sit at his table and experiment with chloroform – there is a famous picture of him and his guests in various stages of intoxication at said table, and under it.

The issues mentioned in "The Athenian Dinner" party are a stark reality, particularly relevant in underdeveloped areas of the world, where they affect millions of women.

Derry O'Dowd is the father-daughter team of Michael and Katy O'Dowd. Michael is an obstetrician gynaecologist, author of *The History of Obstetrics and Gynaecology* (with Elliot E. Philipp), and *The History of Medications for Women: Materia Medica Woman*. Katy spent years working as an arts and entertainment journalist before moving into copywriting, and onto fiction. She is the author of steampunk books *The Lady Astronomer and Memento Mori*.

The first in The Scarlet Ribbon historical fiction series by Derry O'Dowd is available from all good bookshops and at amazon.co.uk/Derry-ODowd.

STEAMPUNK FINLAND

Magdalena Hai
Anne Leinonen
J.S. Meresmaa

Osuuskumma

Osuuskumma is a Finnish co-operative publishing house specialising in all kinds of strange fiction – fantasy, sci-fi, horror, New Weird, steampunk, and the like. Recently we have branched out into international publications under "Osuuskumma International" to offer top-quality Finnish speculative fiction in languages other than Finnish.

Foreword

J.S. Meresmaa

The Age of Finnish Steampunk can be said to have begun in 2012 when the first part of Gigi and Henry trilogy by Magdalena Hai was published. As a small and reclusive northern country in the armpit of Russia, not really a part of Scandinavia and not a part of Eastern Europe either, Finland is a bit of an odd bird. It is not uncommon to have the trends of the wider world land on our doorstep a bit late. Often we miss a trend or two. But sometimes we pick up something that becomes all the rage in a short span of time. Steampunk could be said to be one of those things. Since 2012 a lot has happened: In addition to Hai's trilogy there have been three anthologies, novels, audio short stories and individual short stories published in magazines and e-zines. (And I'm only talking about fiction, here. There's even a steampunk-themed bar in Helsinki.) So you can imagine it wasn't easy to pick just three short stories to represent the Finnish steampunk scene.

The stories I have chosen for this anthology are all from prolific Finnish authors who have also published steampunk in long form. "The Winged Man Isaac" by Magdalena Hai is set in an alternate reality in the late 19th century where a change in the Gulf Stream has partially melted the Greenland Ice Sheet and the Vikings are a major trading power. It shares the same world as her landmark trilogy Gigi and Henry, but it is aimed especially for adult audience. Great in worldbuilding, vast ideas and heavy in emotion it's a fine example of steampunk with Nordic flair.

Masterfully paced, quirky, and full of engineering marvel, "The Cylinder Hat" by Anne Leinonen offers a glimpse of Finnish city life with a twist of black humour. The main character of Siiri's story will reappear in long form as the author is currently working on a novel manuscript that sheds light on parallel realities, and Siiri becomes Iiris.

Lastly, "Augustine" by J.S. Meresmaa, yours truly, features a young girl with bad hearing and high hopes of becoming an engineer. Feminism meets capitalism in a story that takes place in Paris, France in the late 1800s. It is set in the same alternative Europe as the author's trilogy The Ursine Affairs, which introduces a world where some of the great beasts from the last glacial period have survived in the wilds of Siberia and magic exists among the shamanistic tribes.

J.S. Meresmaa
Tampere, Finland
April 2018

The Winged Man Isaac

Magdalena Hai

Translated by Christina Saarinen

If they hadn't harmed the children, everything might have gone differently. Because whenever One-Ear allowed herself to think back to those days, she always thought about the children more than anything. The one Isaac had lost, and the one that was never born.

Sometimes she thought of Isaac, as well.

One-Ear had found him in a trash heap, lying in a foetal position, his upper body covered by a huge mechanical wing. She had cautiously lifted the edge of the wing. On his lower half, the man was wearing clean, sturdy wool pants and leather boots. But instead of a shirt, his upper body was sheathed with strips of metal like talons that wrapped around from back to front and kept a tight grip on his ribcage. The wing let out a metallic creak as One-Ear stretched it upward. The structure was surprisingly stiff, but not heavy. She had a clear view of the man's face as he slept under the wing.

One-Ear stood silently, chewing her shirtsleeve, unable to move.

The sky began to grow light. Somewhere, a child shouted.

The man shuddered. His eyes, blackened by blood and soot, opened. He turned his pained face toward One-Ear.

"Help."

One-Ear wasn't sure how she managed to get the man to the apartment. The stairs leading up to the top floor were narrow, and the man was nearly as limp as the wings dangling from his back, which scraped the walls of the stairwell and got caught on the handrails in the corners. The man was nearly unconscious and scarcely managed to carry his own weight. One-Ear's head felt unnaturally light, too. Her underskirt grew stiff with the blood she had lost, and the rough fabric rubbed mercilessly against her thighs and shins. Convulsions of grief rose up within her, but she forced herself not to think about what had been. The most important thing now was to escape the reach of the spiders.

Isaac awoke. It was late evening, or night. The gas lights of the airships turned the red sky a nauseating yellow. With every movement pain tore through his muscles, but Isaac pulled himself up to sit. He was in a large apartment, from which all the furniture had been removed, apart from the straw-filled, striped mattress he was lying on. The dirty wallpaper hung in shreds from the walls, and the broken windows had let in rain sullied by coal smoke, which had soaked into the floorboards and a twisted rag rug grey with age. In the middle of the floor, a fire place had been built from a few loose bricks. The fire that had once smouldered under a hot plate in an old three-legged pot had gone out, but the iron still radiated heat into the room. There was a dented pot on top of the hot plate. The room smelled like mould and smoke.

Isaac tried to recall what had happened. He remembered a few moments at home, in the workshop. Worrying about Anneliese and Mathilde. The thrilling feeling when the wings that now bit so mercilessly into his back had lifted him into the air, over the rooftops. After that, he had only an indistinct sense of time's passing. Of the days and the nights that slipped past in a torpor. Isaac didn't know how he had ended up here, in this worn-out, grey apartment under a fiery sky.

The door opened with a creak. A mouse-haired young girl came in, thin as a reed under her ragged clothes. The girl barely glanced at him, going instead to the hot plate and lifting the lid of the pot. Steam carried the appetizing scent of barley porridge into the room. Her pale blue eyes glanced thoughtfully at something behind Isaac's shoulder, as if she didn't see him at all. Her narrow lips moved to the rhythm of soundless words. Then, suddenly, the girl's gaze fell on him, and Isaac realised that the girl was not a child, but a young woman. Thin and harrowed-looking, but a woman all the same. She had a symmetrical face, with an attractive plainness. Strikingly high cheekbones. Her tribal features and colouring, vapid like the northern sky, revealed centuries of isolation. Isaac swore silently to himself. A woman with that kind of face... Isaac would be damn lucky if she wasn't a Keloburg Finn.

"Am I your prisoner?" Isaac asked, and then: "Are you a Demon?"

When the woman rose, her mouse-grey hair swung aside for a moment, revealing pink scar tissue where her ear should have been. When she noticed his gaze, she covered her missing ear with her hair.

"They call me One-Ear," she said simply.

"My name is Isaac Beckers," Isaac said, leaning awkwardly on his wings, his chest, marked with deep scrapes, arched painfully forward. "Thank you."

The woman shrugged her shoulders. "Don't thank me yet. I haven't decided what I'm going to do with you."

There were shots somewhere, far in the distance. Hollow, sporadic blasts that bounced repeatedly off the brick walls lining the narrow streets. Isaac saw One-Ear tense to listen and then relax when the shots didn't continue or come closer.

"You didn't answer my question. Are you one of the Demons?" Isaac asked. "Isn't that what you're called around here?"

"No," the woman said. "Not any more."

This wasn't the first time a major accident had occurred in the manufacturing district, of course. The building stock had been replaced at a rapid rate for as long as One-Ear could remember, and they were no strangers to earthquakes caused by the rising land. The great earthquake of 1852, which One-Ear had fortunately only heard about in the stories of older folk, had collapsed an entire section of the city. This time, the earthquake's most powerful wave struck the core of the manufacturing district late in the afternoon. One of the buildings destroyed was the provincial king's giant new textile manufactory. That made matters worse. The actions of Keloburg's aging *huscarl* had long caused discontent among the poorer residents of the city. The friction between the huscarl and the underground movement, which was gaining more and more support, continued to grow. There was much talk about his preference for hiring children over adults, at half pay, and how he forced his underage employees to work days longer than humanly possible. The manufactory was a massive building, constructed of red brick and iron, which sucked into its dusty depths each morning hundreds of workers like a putrid slumbering beast. Of course, the others did the same, and the old Varjag guard held onto their arrogance as avidly as they did their privileges. But King Ingvar, the huscarl, was worst of all. Most of those who had been trapped under the textile factory's roof beams and machinery had been less than fifteen years old. Children who were exhausted through and through and could hardly keep standing, much less run, after a fourteen-hour working day.

The spoon made a sickening screech against the bottom of the pot as One-Ear scooped the porridge into a battered metal plate in the dim gray apartment. From the corner of her eye she saw Isaac stir. He had lost consciousness again.

It was said that the huscarl had been playing fox and geese with his wife when he received word of the accident. He had calmly finished his game before deigning to lift his raunchy backside off his seat. At the same time, the leaders of the underground – a man called Nightingale and his bitch, Niko – had plastered the streets with posters spelling out the old king's sins, from first to last. People said there were as many posters hung as there were dead children in the abyss of the manufactory. Enough to dirty the streets. Enough to set flame to the souls of the poor.

When the riots broke out, the Finns closed the streets with large barrels, passenger cars, and whatever else they could find. Finns Heath, the outlying neighbourhood where they had settled, was located in the far outskirts of the city, adjacent to the sparsely populated Upper Slope and the boggy burial grounds. It was easy to blockade since hardly anyone wanted to travel through the area anyway, especially in times of unrest. The Finns had counted on being too insignificant to either side to be worth drawing into the conflict. After all, what were they in this country, to these people, besides devils and demons? The Finns had a reputation for being skilled at the bucksaw and had been brought to the Isle to fell its forests and fuel the insatiable kilns of the railroads and manufactories. But when the last of the forests around Keloburg had been cut down, the Finns were forgotten, left to fend for themselves. And that's what they did.

Even without the roadblocks they had always been set apart. Different.

One-Ear watched Isaac as he hovered at the edge of consciousness. At times he was delirious; at times he talked in his sleep, and One-Ear listened. A plan began to take shape in her mind. When the man was awake, One-Ear fed him barley gruel, skimping on the kernels. He had a good appetite though it clearly hurt him to eat. The wings, constructed of metal and leather, stretched out behind his back like a fan, their surface occasionally reflecting the flash of firebombs as delicate flecks of light on the grey walls of the apartment. One-Ear considered cleaning the open wounds on the man's chest, but there were so many that she was afraid she would hurt him more than she could help him. One-Ear was no doctor. But perhaps there was something she could do for him.

After he had eaten, the man fell asleep with his head hanging against his shoulder. One-Ear took the shawl from her shoulders and folded it under his head for a pillow. Then she drew from her pocket a set of crescent wrenches and screwdrivers.

When the unrest began, the decision to close Finns Heath was made by consensus, and both the Varjags and the underground were notified. The Demons, along with the rest of their tribe, had sworn to keep the line. No one was allowed inside the borders.

But the riots had continued and spread, turning into a violent, uncontrollable uprising and, finally, full-fledged urban warfare. Firebombs fell closer and closer to the area where the Finns lived. One-Ear had feared it was only a matter of time before they would be drawn into the conflict. All it would take was some small spark, a rumour or misinformation claiming they sympathised with the rebels, and they too would be swallowed up by war.

The remains of the destroyed manufactories had been smouldering for three weeks when the Demons mistakenly took custody of a Varjag at a roadblock. One-Ear had protested when Matias decided to take the man with them, but for one reason or another her demands had fallen on deaf ears. Matias was the third to have led the Demons. Before him had been Juhani Korpela, who was hanged for killing a man, and before that Laura, who was called Iron-Hand and had originally established the street gang called the Demons. One-Ear didn't know what had happened to Laura, but both of her daughters had been members of the Demons from birth. Tilda had started a family and left the gang, but the younger daughter, Liisa, was still heavily involved. Liisa was moody and quick to use her fists, and One-Ear was afraid of her. They had all been satisfied when Matias took control of the gang after Juhani got himself hanged. Under Matias, the number of Demons had grown from about thirty to a hundred and now included nearly all of the younger people in Finns Heath.

Back at headquarters, One-Ear had climbed on top of an old trunk and crossed her legs in front of her. The mound of her belly was growing day by day, preventing her from lifting her knees under her chin as she would have liked. She rubbed the underside of her stomach protectively. The pregnancy hadn't been planned or wanted, but just a short while ago, One-Ear had started to feel a delicate fluttering, like the brush of a feather. At first, they had puzzled her, but now she realized she was secretly looking forward to the little nudges.

There wasn't a sound to be heard from the lower city. The explosions had dropped off during the day. One-Ear tried to imagine the scene on the other side of the roadblock. Collapsed buildings and, between them, small points of fire. Bodies mangled by spiders and bullets, that no one had cleared away. Perhaps the residents were focused on putting out fires. The rebel fighters would have retreated to cellars and caves under the city; an expansive underground network now covered nearly all of the Lowlands. Hundreds of feet above them, the Varjagian airships floated silently and threateningly, like thunderclouds.

The air felt oppressive – as if it too was waiting for something to happen.

One-Ear stared at the Varjag lying on the floor of the hut. A group of men in civilian clothing had come in the dark of night and tried to penetrate the area by force. How could they have known? Everything had happened so suddenly. When the fight was over, the Demons had found among the corpses a man just barely alive. He was sprawled alongside the roadblock with blood spurting from the corner of his mouth. The Demons had dragged the man to headquarters for questioning, and only when they stripped off his jacket did they notice the two-headed snake of Keloburg tattooed on his forearm.

"Soldier," Matias said. "God damn."

"Judging from his fingernails, he's no rank-and-file," Liisa said from where she squatted next to the man. "An officer and a gentleman," she spat and let the man's hand fall.

"We should have left him there," One-Ear said again, tearing a hangnail from next to her thumb.

Matias glanced at her and snorted.

Liisa looked up from beside the man. "Who the hell is this guy? And why were they trying to get into Finns Heath? We don't have anything here."

Iiris picked at the knobbly pulls on her shirtsleeves. Her eyes, wide with fear, moved from the man to Matias and One-Ear in turn. "Maybe we could get a ransom for him."

The girl's mouth was a soft, round fruit, and One-Ear knew that Matias kissed it stealthily each night. As far as she was concerned, they could just as well have done it in the open. Though the child she was carrying was Matias', One-Ear had never believed that he loved her or wanted her for a wife. Matias meant nothing to her, and Iiris was her friend.

When Iiris spoke, One-Ear saw relief and hope in the Demons' eyes, which were immediately dashed by a barely discernible shake of Matias's head.

"He's waking up!" Liisa hissed and bounded further away from the man. "Hand me a pitchfork!"

The gang of Demons grew tense. Someone brought out a knife that had been hidden in the folds of his clothing, another grabbed a wooden club from against the wall. Penni threw a pitchfork to Liisa, who caught it deftly and swung its sharp tines toward the man. The teeth of the fork pressed down a hair above his collarbone, on the white skin that lay exposed under the collar of his shirt.

The man groaned and opened his eyes. He had brown, grown-out hair and the tidy beard and sideburns of a gentleman. There was a cut at the corner of his nose, and his lip was swollen and bloody, but anyone passing him on a city street on a normal day would have said he had a pleasant face. The face of a gentleman, One-Ear found herself thinking – and corrected herself immediately, because his eyes were cruelly calculating.

"What's happened?" the man said, his voice coarse with blood. "My men..."

Matias stepped forward. "We found you in the street," he

lied with the quick braggadocio of a former guttersnipe. "You're lucky Rat found you at all."

Rat sneered; his gums, white with scurvy, gleamed.

"Otherwise you could have ended up in the wrong hands, unconscious like that." Matias smiled generously, but the soldier didn't smile back. He seemed to be considering his options.

"Clearly there has been a misunderstanding," the man said. He spoke the musical Varjagian dialect of the Hills, but its melody was tarnished by the coarseness of his words. "I know who you are, and I know you don't want to get mixed up in our affairs. If you know what's best for you, you'll return me to my people."

One-Ear saw the man grope for support to pull himself to his feet, but either the pitchfork's teeth, which Liisa pressed more firmly against him, or the discomfort induced by the earlier assault stopped his efforts short.

"You know who we are, but we don't know you. Who are you, and what are you doing in Finns Heath?" Matias threw off his good cop mask as quickly as he had put it on.

"Nothing that has anything to do with the Demons."

"Everything that goes on in these streets has something to do with us."

The man considered his next words. "All right. I'm looking for a certain man. If you help me find him, we can forget this..." The man glanced at the fork tines pressed against his throat. "Misunderstanding."

"It depends. Is the man a Finn?" Matias asked.

"A Dutchman," the man replied. "He may be injured, or dead."

"Why?"

"He was seen falling the night before last somewhere in the area of Finns Heath."

"Falling? There aren't any airships over Finns Heath – and there haven't been any," Matias said, furrowing his brow.

The Varjag looked unsure for a moment how much he

should tell the Finns. "He didn't fall from an airship. He was traveling alone... The man has mechanical wings on his back."

Liisa snorted a laugh. "This bloke is looking for an angel among the Demons!"

The Demons never found out the man's identity or whether he could get them off the hook for the death of his soldiers. That night, the man was struck with a high fever. He lay in the middle of the floor, trembling helplessly, but none of the Demons were willing to come close enough to even cover him with a blanket.

"If he dies," Rat said, echoing aloud what everyone was secretly thinking, "then we can get rid of the body without causing a stir and pretend we don't know anything about him."

"Why wait?" Liisa said, reminding One-Ear, again, why she stayed away from her. "We can always hurry things along..." Liisa drew a slow line across her throat with her forefinger.

Matias shook his head. "We've talked about this. We're done with those kinds of games. After what happened to Juhani... You don't want to go back to those days, do you?"

The Demons shook their heads. It wasn't just a matter of not wanting to cross certain lines. Many of them still remembered the days when Juhani Korpela had been their leader. Violence had been a constant, even within the gang. In the end, Juhani got caught and was quickly convicted. One-Ear had seen a picture of Juhani's hanging in the paper and had secretly been glad. Things were better since Matias had taken over. The Demons were feared, but at least they didn't have to fear each other.

The Varjag started to vomit blood and mucus during the night, and by morning the man lay dead on the floor of the hut. The Demons buried him deep in a bog eye on the edge of Finns Heath. But by that point the game had already been lost. Someone had seen something, someone had told. When word reached the Varjags, the government's retaliation was efficient and ruthless. Finns Heath was declared a rebel area. The many-legged black steam tanks called spiders levelled the roadblocks as if they had been made of matchsticks. And most people hadn't stuck around to fight. They had either fled or been mangled by the legs of the spiders.

Afterwards, One-Ear had left to search for the winged man. Bloody, alone, and half-crazed with rage and grief, all she knew was that she wouldn't hand the man over to the Varjags.

Isaac felt the air flow under his wings. His whole body ached. Unyielding, rending, deeply penetrating waves of pain pumped strength into the savaged tissues of his upper body. Pain flashed before his eyes in glowing, white balls of light, but Isaac paid them no attention; instead he sliced again and again through the cushion of warm air radiating from below. Despite Bruno's efforts to deter him, he had set out as soon as his muscles had recovered enough to carry him to his destination. As afternoon turned to evening, he crossed the mountains and at last saw the city of Keloburg before him. The mass of buildings and its many shades of brown were obscured in places by a thick, black curtain of smoke. Some of the buildings had collapsed, leaving gaps in the pleated rows of multi-storeyed buildings. Everything about the city looked dirty and repellent in Isaac's eyes. Before him floated government airships.

Isaac awoke groggily and wasn't sure whether it was the same day as before. The apartment was empty; the woman who had called herself One-Ear had left. Something soft brushed Isaac's shoulder. Isaac fumbled the fabric hanging on his wing and yanked at it. His wing shook, sending a hot wave of pain through his body, and he groaned through clenched teeth. When the pain receded, he took a closer look at the wad of cloth in his hand. It was a loosely knit piece of fabric, its blue and green checks faded and fuzzy. There was a hole near the edge where some screw or other part of Isaac's wing had caught on the fabric. Isaac pushed his finger through the hole. The mouse-haired woman's shawl. A sudden impulse drove Isaac to press the fabric against his face and breathe in its scent. It smelled like a woman, like vanilla, and vaguely bitter. The scent made him miss Anneliese more than ever.

The memories returned. And when they came they burned him to the core.

Isaac's head had fallen forwards, his massive wings arced out on either side of his mangled torso, his hands rested in his lap. One-Ear crouched besidehim, laid the bundle she was carrying on the ground, and touched his cheek. It was warm, but no longer hot. The man's eyelids flickered at her touch. He held One-Ear's shawl in his hands. When One-Ear tried to take her shawl back, Isaac awoke and gripped the fabric with both hands as if it would protect him. When his panic and confusion subsided, Isaac opened his clenched fingers.

"It's got a hole in it," he said, showing her the spot in the blue-green fabric. "I'm sorry."

One-Ear didn't reveal her irritation. Without saying a word, she tied the shawl back around her shoulders, bent down over her bundle, and opened the strings that held it together.

"I thought you abandoned me," Isaac said.

"I brought food."

Inside the bundle were a piece of bread and some leathery vegetables. Carrots, potatoes, an onion. Isaac kept awake the entire time it took One-Ear to light the fire and bring water to a boil. He watched how she cut the potatoes and carrots into pieces and sliced the onion. One-Ear was sorry to no longer have any seasonings. Isaac shrugged his shoulders. It seemed to One-Ear that the man's pain had lessened somewhat while she was away.

When the potatoes had softened, One-Ear took the pot from the stove.

"Can I ask you something?" Isaac said suddenly. His gaze was direct and serious. "Why are you helping me?"

He was trying to catch her eye, but One-Ear pretended she hadn't noticed. She couldn't tell Isaac about her plan. About the talons she had constructed while he slept, or about the *Ormen Lange*. He wasn't ready.

"Eat," One-Ear said. "Get your strength back."

Isaac and One-Ear spent the next days alone in the desolate attic apartment. One-Ear mostly stayed in the apartment, but from time to time she went out and brought back more food and water. She prepared a thick salve of plantain leaves, resin, and other ingredients that remained unknown to Isaac, which she applied to Isaac's wounds. Her nimble fingers felt cool against Isaac's skin.

"They go all the way in," Isaac said. He had watched her eyes, how her gaze wandered over his chest. "The wings are anchored to me, and I to them. We're one being."

Her fingers paused. She glanced at Isaac, unable to fully conceal her shock. She set the cup of plantain salve on the floor and looked closely, as if for the first time, at the harness Isaac bore, and not merely his wings. She laid her hand on Isaac's chest and traced the edges of the metal claws on his bare skin.

"But how?"

One-Ear saw metal where there should have been unbroken skin. Fresh scar tissue, which she had assumed were caused by his fall. Wounds that had scarcely healed and had then opened again when he struck the earth.

One-Ear raised her eyes to his face. "Who did this to you?"

"I did it to myself. Or, at least, I ordered it done."

The wings behind him, leaning against the wall, were shaped like those of a bird, but their feathers were made of metal and leather. Now he had folded them closed, but when stretched to their full extent, the span of each wing was several meters. One-Ear's eyes drifted back to the metal claws that gripped the man's chest. The strips of skin visible between them were red and swollen from the pressure of the claws. One-Ear ran her finger cautiously along the surface of the skin and tried to understand – in a mixture of wonder and admiration – the cruelty of the construction.

Wounded. That was the word that described the woman best in Isaac's mind. Not fragile or weak. But definitely wounded. Anneliese had become like that, too, when Mathilde was taken. She had looked as though nothing could ever hurt her any more than that.

Mathilde and her friend Gert had been fishing in a stream alongside the main road. Most of the time, all that could be had from the small stream was trash fish and minnows, but locals said they would sometimes catch a salmon. Salmon was what the girls were hoping for, too. When Isaac and his family had moved to the small village that had been built for migrant workers about thirty kilometres northwest of Keloburg, they had been assured that the area was safe and the people were friendly. Neither Isaac and Anneliese nor Gertrude's parents had thought to worry about their children's absence until the evening. Only when the girls didn't show up for dinner did they realise that something was wrong.

Anneliese' brother, Bruno, had led the search party. They found out that Mathilde and her friend had fallen into the hands of government men.

"It was one of the groups of mercenaries headed toward Keloburg," Bruno told them when he returned to the house. "The high king sent them to help the huscarl put down the rebellion. They're savages, Isaac. The peasants say the high king looks the other way and gives the mercenaries liberties not allowed regular soldiers. When a band of them passes, the peasants lower their eyes and shut their daughters indoors, if they manage in time. They think the girls were taken to Keloburg," Bruno said sombrely. "To the pleasure corps. I'm sorry, Isaac."

"There must be a mistake," Isaac said. "We're here as their guests!"

"We're foreigners, Isaac. The Varjags don't care about us. They never have," Bruno said. "When it comes down to it, we're the same scum in their eyes as the rebels in Keloburg."

Isaac refused to believe his brother-in-law's words. "Mathilde is only 13 years old! Just a child," he sputtered.

Anneliese withdrew to her rooms – not to grieve, but to extinguish herself with grief. She stopped eating and drinking, and merely lay in bed with dry, gaping eyes, clutching Mathilde's nightshirt against her chest. Isaac had refused to give up. He had sent an urgent message by courier to the provincial king, but from the lack of response they understood that the Varjags didn't intend to return the girl. The rebels had made surprising gains in the city, and even outside Keloburg there was talk of a state of war rather than a rebellion; the Varjags of Keloland had neither time for nor interest in dealing with the troubles of a landless migrant worker.

The anguish and distress in Anneliese' eyes had driven Isaac to his decision. He would get Mathilde back himself.

"Are you crazy, Isaac? The high king's troops have surrounded Keloburg," Bruno said. "You'll never make it to the city."

"I'll make it if I go over the mountains," Isaac said, shaking his head. "The Varjags cut off Precipice Pass to the south of the city, but they aren't expecting anyone to come over the mountains."

"You mean you'll fly?" Bruno asked. "Even if you could get your hands on a one-man airship, its hull would be so big you'd be detected as soon as you got close to Keloburg, day or night. You'd be shot down."

In response, Isaac spread in front of them on the table two wide rolls of paper that he had pulled out of the large cabinet in his office.

Bruno paled when he saw Isaac's plans. "Isaac, this is madness! The change is permanent. I'm not willing to do that to you."

"Don't you see how your sister is suffering?" Isaac shouted. "Do you want to lose Anneliese along with Mathilde? I'm the one taking the risk here, not you."

Bruno rubbed his temples and stared at the diagrams. "I... I won't –"

"Do it."

Bruno had laboured three days sawing, cutting, attaching flesh to metal while Isaac lay in a morphine coma. When his work was complete, Bruno, horrified at what he had done, destroyed the plans and any trace of the wings so that no one else would ever suffer the same fate. When Isaac awoke, he had become Anneliese's delivering angel.

A winged man.

Isaac wept. He didn't know when he had started weeping, or why, but he sobbed miserably, wordlessly, like a small child. Words poured out of him in rivulets and in rapids. When he finally stopped, he realised he was leaning on the woman's pigeon chest, nearly lying in the embrace of her slender arms. One-Ear had drawn him against herself.

Tears streamed down One-Ear's neck, filling the cavity between her collarbones and soaking into the front of her dress. The coolness of the day raised goose bumps on the flesh of her breasts. One-Ear stroked the man's hair and cradled his head in her arms. The gesture was instinctive, motherly, but when the man's crying had subsided and the involuntary tremors of his body had ceased, his breathing remained shallow. The sudden awareness of the closeness of another made One-Ear's body tense, taut as a bow. When the man's warm lips pressed against the tender skin of her collarbones, One-Ear moaned. Isaac interpreted the sound and her movement as a sign of consent. His palm grazed her breast; his finger brushed the place that had grown firm under her shirt.

One-Ear drew in a breath.

Isaac lifted her skirt clumsily, as if he feared losing everything should he slow down or let go. One-Ear was surprised to find herself opening her thighs to him, surrendering to his embrace.

The man's hands were strong and rugged. Isaac wanted to kiss her, and One-Ear, astonished, returned his kiss, tasting the salty tears on his lips. Their taste made One-Ear's body soften, receptive to Isaac's hands.

"I want to know your name," Isaac murmured against her lips. "I can't call you One-Ear now."

"Johanna," One-Ear said quietly. "My name is Johanna."

Isaac rose to his knees, bearing One-Ear in his arms. One-Ear felt a rush of air as the metal wings beat in the confines of the cramped apartment. Isaac whispered her name.

"You've lost a child, too." Isaac said it with certainty.

One-Ear stood at the window, watching the red sky. When One-Ear spoke, Isaac heard Anneliese's anguish in her voice. "How can one city burn for so long?"

Isaac slowly brought himself to his feet. The weight of the wings still racked his chest, but the wounds that had opened up when he hit the ground were starting to heal. As Isaac walked, the wings responded to his movements, their gleaming copper tips raising a trail of swirling dust in his wake. Isaac wrapped his arms around One-Ear and pressed against her back.

"Tell me," Isaac whispered.

Isaac felt again the tension in One-Ear's body.

"It was just a baby," she said, staring out the window. "Not even that. But I already thought of it as a baby. I could feel it moving." She placed her hands on her belly, which was flat and empty. One-Ear forced her face and voice to keep steady. "They captured us soon after someone revealed the location of our headquarters. Me and Iiris. The government troops..." She shut her eyes and shook her head. "Matias – he was my baby's father – he heard us shouting. He tried to stop the soldiers, but there was nothing he could do by himself. They threw him to the ground. They pushed his face into a puddle outside the hut and held him under the water until he stopped struggling."

One-Ear was surprised how impassively she could already

think of the events of that day. As if they had happened to someone else, who was now speaking through her. Someone else had witnessed her friends' death and torture, someone else had felt the kicks of the soldier's boot, taken on her rounded belly as she lay helpless at the men's feet.

"I lost my baby, its father, and my best friend. Iiris was always the most beautiful of us. They took her with them. Me they didn't want, looking like this." One-Ear pointed to the scar tissue on the side of her head and shrugged her shoulders. "It's what saved me. The miscarriage made my slit bleed much more than Iiris's. My whole body was shaking. They probably thought I would die anyway, there in the mud next to Matias. Liisa Iron-Hand died fighting. I don't know about the others. None of us were willing to take the lead after that. We all ran off in different directions."

"How long ago was that?"

One-Ear wrinkled her brow and rubbed her forehead with her fingers, irritated. "I found you soon afterward."

"Do you think that your friend is still...?" Isaac asked.

One-Ear shook her head. "No. She was a Demon, too."

"I'm sorry," Isaac said.

"He was looking for you," One-Ear said without looking at Isaac. "That Varjag that died. That the Demons were destroyed over."

Isaac didn't answer right away.

The clamour and crunching of heavy metallic legs sounded nearby, and they pulled back from the window, deeper into the shadows. But the machine moved quickly on, out of earshot.

Isaac began to speak in a monotone: "Bruno and I and several others of our countrymen were invited here as engineers for the air force. The offer was generous and included the upkeep of our families. I was made director of the research division. The Varjags already had large-class Gregorovian airships, but they wanted me to design machines that would be fast, small, and suitable for close combat. They wanted something unique, something no one else had." Isaac smiled at the dwindling memory. "I came up with these wings after a night of drinking. I didn't honestly believe that they could be of use to anyone. I didn't think anyone would be crazy enough to..." Isaac fell silent.

"Something went wrong on your virgin flight," One-Ear said. "I repaired your wing while you were unconscious. Your brother-in-law fastened the shoulder joints poorly, and they didn't hold up under the stress of the long flight."

Isaac stared at One-Ear's delicate shoulders in front of him. "You're an excellent mechanic." Isaac had noticed that the wings were moving better, but he hadn't known that he had her to thank for it.

"It was my responsibility in the Demons," One-Ear said, as if she were speaking of something that had happened long ago and was no longer of any consequence. She pointed to the sky. Several government airships circled over the lower city, hellish things like giant dung beetles lit by gas lamps. "They brought their main fleet here after the underground managed to occupy the central railway station and declared Keloburg a free city," One-Ear said. "Do you see those cables, with their tops hidden in the clouds? The elevator baskets that move along them?"

Isaac nodded.

"The *Ormen Lange* is hovering there," One-Ear said. "The pleasure craft the high king of Godtborg built for his troops. It descends lower when they take a fresh batch of girls aboard. Before that, they throw the previous ones away. It's a dirty war tactic they use to break the resistance and demoralize the rebels."

"Good Lord." Isaac stared at the clouds churning over the city.

"I've seen girls falling over the bulwarks more than once," One-Ear said.

Isaac's thoughts returned to the moment he heard of Mathilde's disappearance. The hours he had lain on the operating table, worked on by Bruno; the time he had taken to recover from the operation; and finally, to the days in this apartment, of which he had no memory. "How long was I unconscious? How long did I lie here?"

One-Ear pulled herself from his embrace and turned toward him, but was unable to look him in the eye. "Who knows? The days drag by here and always look the same. A few weeks, maybe a month?"

Isaac gasped and braced himself against the wall.

"I'm sorry, Isaac," One-Ear said. "No one lasts that long on the pleasure craft."

Isaac felt the earth heave and gasped for air in an effort to maintain consciousness. The faces of Mathilde and Anneliese as he remembered them from happier days appeared in grotesque flashes before his eyes. As if through a haze, Isaac heard One-Ear say slowly, half to herself, "There's more. Before the Demons were destroyed, there was talk in the city that the underground had received the support of certain entities in Europe whose goal was to break the dominance of the Varjags in the North Atlantic."

Isaac shook his head. "But we don't have anything to do with... We don't..."

"I've thought about what the dead Varjag said," One-Ear continued mercilessly. "He called you a Dutchman. He knew who you were. Someone must have noticed you'd left and sent word to Keloburg. If your wings had carried you, you might have made it to the city before anyone betrayed your departure. You might have even found out where they were holding your daughter. But now... The Varjags will consider your coming here a crime, the act of a foreign agent."

The room spun before Isaac's eyes and he sank to his knees on the floor. One-Ear crouched down beside him, stroked the hair of his temple, and said, "Your family is dead, Isaac. All you have left is revenge."

They made love again that night, clinging to each other in a frenzy. They woke long before sunrise, and One-Ear told Isaac what he needed to do to cause as much destruction as possible.

Isaac rolled his head as if in pain, but One-Ear brought him around again and again. With strong leather straps she bound to his arms the long metal talons she had constructed for him to wield. She led Isaac to the roof and kissed him goodbye.

"Do it for Mathilde," One-Ear said. "For all the loved ones you've lost."

When he had gone, One-Ear took a deep breath.

"To you, unborn one, I offer this sacrifice," One-Ear whispered, stroking her empty belly. "So you know you aren't forgotten. So you know I haven't forgiven them."

Isaac made use of air currents to fly higher and higher toward the airships. Not a single shot was fired. No one noticed when Isaac attached himself like a large bat or an eagle with hands to the hull of the slowly descending personnel ship. One-Ear saw how the creature – she couldn't think of it as Isaac any longer – started to tear the envelope of the ship to shreds with its long talons, striking again and again, furiously, desperately, until the hull gave way. Then the creature pulled loose the piece of fabric draped across its chest and set it aflame. The burning scrap of cloth disappeared into the depths of the ship.

As the creature took flight again, an explosive blue and red inferno surged out of the ship's hull. The hot burst of air tossed the creature about like a leaf in the wind. The airship began to cant dangerously to the left. The roar of the fire could be heard all the way from the rooftop where One-Ear stood. She watched expressionlessly as small black figures jumped from the airship to their death. The airship tumbled into chaos. It drifted over the river and plunged ablaze into the centre of the city's bourgeois quarter, a fiery slice of hell the size of an apartment building.

One-Ear refused to feel guilty for the deaths of the girls who were still on the ship as it fell. Not even for the fact that she may have exaggerated when she told Isaac how long he had lain unconscious. Who knew, maybe it would have still been possible to rescue his daughter from the *Ormen Lange*. But One-Ear would not feel guilt. She had decided as much when she lay bleeding, her face in the mud and a stillborn child at her feet. She had sworn that she would find the strength and the means. She had to regroup the Demons and meet them as the leader they needed. Because of Isaac, it had become clear to her that her time in power wouldn't be like Matias', and neither would she be a new Juhani Korpela. In One-Ear's trained mind, every detail of the metal wings, every screw and joint, shone clear and bright as if the construction were still before her eyes.

One-Ear understood machines. It would be easy to reconstruct the wings. She also understood the sacrifices the new age would demand of the Demons, and she knew they were equal to them. Standing on the roof of the abandoned building, watching Keloburg burn, she swore on her still-born child's grave that airships would never again blanket the sky over Keloburg like storm clouds, and that not a single child of theirs would die at the hands of the Varjags. The reign of Johanna One-Ear would be remembered as the time when the Demons earned a new name for themselves. This would be the beginning of the age of Angels, when the city's rooftops would be governed by her creations.

The creature that had been Isaac died in an outburst of flame. One-Ear never went to look for the body.

Magdalena Hai is a Finnish author of SF&F. Her first novel *Kerjäläisprinsessa (The Beggar Princess)* was released in 2012, starting the appraised steampunk trilogy Gigi & Henry, to be followed by *Kellopelikuningas (The Clockwork King)* and *Susikuningatar (The Wolf Queen)*. Hai's prose, long and short, has won several awards, including the Atorox Award (2016) and Finnish Literary Export Prize (2018). Her children's book *Kurnivamahainen kissa (The*

Grumblebelly Cat) was nominated in March 2018 for the prestigious Nordic Council Children and Young People's Literature Prize. Her short stories have been translated previously into English, Spanish, and Estonian. A lover of cross genre and all things strange, Hai's fiction often combines elements of sci-fi, fantasy and horror. Besides writing, Hai is an active member and editor at Osuuskumma Publishing.

The Cylinder Hat

Anne Leinonen

Translated by Christina Saarinen

Siiri

Siiri opened the vestibule door. Behind it stood a young gentleman in a black jacket with a laugh in his eyes.

"There was something particular I was supposed to say, but now I can't remember," the man said, looking Siiri in the eye. "Here's this, anyway."

Siiri curtsied and sputtered a greeting. Who on Earth was this man, and what was he doing at her mistress' door? There had certainly been plenty of peculiar gentlemen calling at Mrs. Viljakainen's house, but generally they went directly to the door of the shop, not around to the service entrance.

"Take it, now," the man said, holding out a black top hat with both hands. Siiri took it without another thought. She ran her fingers along the hat's surface. It was covered in silk, there was a terrible dent at one temple, and there seemed to be a stain on the brim.

"I'll be going," the man said, raising his hand to his brim and turning away from Siiri.

"But... " Siiri reached out after the man, but he stepped purposefully towards the street. Siiri was bewildered. For a brief moment it felt as if the man's visit was somehow both significant and familiar. Déjà vu.

When she went back inside, Mrs. Viljakainen had woken up and was stumbling on her thick legs to the kitchen door.

"Who was that?" she asked.

"I don't know. A young gentleman. He brought this. Does it belong to some outfit?"

Mrs. Viljakainen humphed. "I only make hats for women. Maybe it was meant for you," she said. "Maybe a suitor."

"A suitor? Surely you would have warned me about something like that?" Siiri asked uncertainly.

The old woman laughed. "The universe warns us when it will," she said. "Empty the chamber pot and prepare breakfast. We don't have all day."

Siiri did as she was told. Mrs. Viljakainen had treated Siiri well ever since the day she read the introductory letter that Siiri's mother had prepared and agreed to hire her. For the sake of kin, she had said, but Siiri had seen something else in the woman's eyes, too. The woman had seemed to see through her, as she did again now. It was rumoured she had the skills of a soothsayer, and indeed, Siiri had sometimes heard her predict the future. But Siiri wasn't expecting a suitor – she was awaiting her brother Veerti. Siiri had promised to look after her little brother, and a familiar itch in her nose told her something was up. Veerti was a teller of tales and had a tendency to get himself into trouble. Could he have been kicked out of his boarding house or ended up in trouble with the bailiff?

Siiri took care of the morning chores as she had been instructed, cleaned up after breakfast, and checked in on the shop side to see that everything was in order. Her mistress designed custom clothing – elegant dresses and shawls. The work itself was done by hired seamstresses. Mrs. Viljakainen occasionally stepped in to produce a complicated bit of embroidery or bodice. It was Siiri's responsibility to ensure that everything was ready for the day's work.

On her way back to her own room, Siiri saw the top hat on the table in the hall where she had left it. She picked up the hat and turned it in her hands, examining it. Inside the hat she found the manufacturer's tag. Hermandorff, it read.

Siiri knew the shop. It was right in the centre of the city. She could stop in when she went to the market for fresh vegetables. Maybe the hat maker would know who the hat should be returned to.

Master von Hermandorff

After the girl had laid the hat on the counter and left, the master sighed and wiped his bald head. How was it possible for the hat to appear like this on his counter? The hat was the work of his own hands, he was sure of that. And it was heavy, too. Stronger and sturdier than usual. The master turned the hat over and knocked on the base from the inside. Then he took his knife and pressed it carefully into the seam between the crown tip and the cylinder. He carefully pried the seam apart and removed the crown tip lining. Underneath was a second, thinner lining, which hid behind it all kinds of cogs and balance wheels – tiny masterworks of precision engineering that he had hidden within the hat when he made it.

He squinted and shook his head. Sometimes it was hard to think. . . What had he been doing? Ah. Yes, the hat was one of his own, one of his prototypes! But it looked strange indeed. Had he really managed to fit so many mechanisms inside? Cylinders, pistons, magnet wire, moving contacts, small field magnets... How did it go, again? He had the plans, they must be here. He went through the papers strewn around his desk but didn't find a single one that even slightly resembled the mechanism in front of him.

He rose from his stool and walked to the back room, where his most important handiworks were set on a shelf in a row. He counted them, one by one. Yes, there were only six top hats. The seventh was missing.

The missing hat must be the one that had just been brought to him. But how had it ended up in the hands of that girl? In fact, how had it ended up anywhere? It had been here the whole time, under lock and key, and he had counted the hats carefully every evening. What's more, the hat that had been returned was the latest in the series, the one he had worked on most recently. Just yesterday, if he remembered correctly.

He pulled a stool from under the workbench, sat, and removed from his belt a handful of instruments, pliers, and screwdrivers. He put the loupe to his eye and checked that every cog, cylinder, and balance wheel was in its place. His instinct and experience told him they were, but at the same time he was delighted at what he saw, as if he were discovering forgotten aspects of his own work. That balance wheel! So skillfully placed! He had built and polished the parts himself, and hundreds, if not thousands, of hours of work had gone into them.

He opened another hat, and a third, and had to admit that this runaway hat truly was more advanced than his earlier models. The first in the series contained a shoddy regular watch mechanism. But the latest model, which had just returned home, was something entirely new. How was that possible? He couldn't say, because he didn't remember creating it.

Finally, he straightened the dent in the side band and wiped away the blood stain. Now the hat was as good as new.

He placed the hat back on the shelf and admired it. Now he remembered. It had all come to him at night. A compulsion to make the hats and to build inside them a particular kind of mechanism. In a dream he had seen how the parts would be laid out, and, when he awoke, he remembered it clearly, which was uncommon. Usually he didn't remember his dreams at all.

The hat's mechanism was brilliant, inspired. It had to be – it was his work, wasn't it? He burst into laughter and wiped the sweat from his brow. Something big and meaningful would come of this yet. Everyone would know his name – he would be famous!

Veerti

He had chosen the shop carefully. Iiris, who cleaned the place in the evenings, had informed him that most of the time her boss was either senselessly drunk or kicking up a din over nothing.

"He's sniffed too much of his own poisons," Iiris said. "He says the strangest things. You'd think he were doing work for the Devil himself..."

That suited Veerti just fine. It wasn't his first time at this kind of thing. And if the shopkeeper was drunk enough, it could be some time before the deed was noticed, broadening the cast of suspects and making it harder to find clues.

He had got his hands on Iiris's key, pressed it into a bar of soap, and cast an identical key from metal.

And today was the day to take action. When the clock struck twelve and the owner was presumably at the dinner table, Veerti went to try his key in the lock. He checked that no one was watching, slipped the key into the lock, and turned. Worked like a charm. He had inquired about the layout and organisation of the rooms while gallivanting with Iiris. Iiris had also told him about her boss' practice of stashing his rainy-day fund in the workshop. The master was a penny-pincher, keeping the money he received from customers in a chest of drawers. Veerti was experienced in these things and opened it easily. A heavy purse slipped into his breast pocket. Drawer closed, padlock in place, and the shopkeeper wouldn't notice a thing.

A neat row of stylish hats stood on a shelf. Veerti couldn't resist the temptation and grabbed the one in the middle. When he had gone a few blocks away from the shop, he threw his own billycock aside and placed the top hat on his head. With it on, he looked just like a tycoon. His jacket wasn't nearly as dapper, but he would get a new one from the tailor straight away.

Actually, he could go to Siiri's place now and take his sister shopping. There were all sorts of things she had wanted so badly, such as some beautiful muslin cloth, but they had never had money for things like that. Now they would, and Siiri would be so happy.

Suddenly he felt a strange sensation. It was as if the world had shattered to pieces in front of his eyes. Some kind of vision problem, maybe? Perhaps it was yesterday's moonshine still pressing on the back his eyes, or maybe he was losing his sight, like his granddad, who had spent his last years completely blind and dependent on the charity of others.

Veerti laughed. He saw himself in a stylish suit surrounded by young ladies, each more lovely than the next. The bank president shook his hand and congratulated Veerti on the manor he had just bought for himself. Out of the corner of his eye he saw a glimpse of his previous life: his mother's tired eyes; the wretched pants patched three times over; Eeverti from next door beating his calves with a stick. Never again, never...

One, two, three... impossible things, worlds that pressed in on his perception in a continuous stream.

In one, he walked on the right side of the street, and in another, on the left.

In one, he didn't go into the hatter's shop, no, and he didn't get hit by a car... Veerti laughed. Where did that car come from with its steam a-puffing? Little by little his vision sharpened, but he still looked at the world as if through a fly's eyes.

He lurched into the street, not noticing the chimney-bus approaching him at speed from the right.

At the last moment he realised it was the hat that had obscured his vision, though it sounded odd: how could you lose your sight to a hat? And then it was too late.

Oskari

"Nothing ever happens around here," Oskari had just said to his friend when they heard a crunch. In an instant, a crowd of astonished onlookers formed a wall in front of the spot where the accident had occurred. Oskari tried to peer through the crowd, but the adults were big and blocked his view. But their muttered words fuelled his imagination.

"He walked right in front of the bus!"

"No, the other fellow pushed him."

"What other fellow? There was only one."

"That man with the hat shoved him."

"What man with the hat?"

A gap opened up in the mass of people, and Oskari got a glimpse of the accident. The man's head had been crushed under a wheel.

"Oh gosh," Oskari gasped. For once, something was happening!

He noticed a hat lying a few yards from the wall of people. An elegant, black gentleman's hat. He went over and picked it up. He turned it in his hands. There was a dent at the temple, and next to that a stain that left a red smudge on his thumb.

Father would like the hat very much. Or even better, he could sell it at the market and get money for it. It would look well on Oskari, too, though it was a bit big. He traced the edge of the brim with his hand and stroked the hat with his thumb. He was about to place it on his head when a heavy hand fell on his shoulder and took hold of the hat's brim.

"You scoundrel, where did you get this from?"

Squirm as he might, Oskari couldn't escape the man's grip.

"I'll take this," the man said. Oskari broke free and ran off as fast as his legs would carry him.

Heikki

When Heikki held the top hat, his fingertips began to tingle, and the feeling spread like wildfire up to his elbows. Heikki wrinkled his brow. For a fleeting moment, he had felt as if he should recognize the little boy from somewhere, but the feeling was gone as soon as it came. Maybe he had run into the kid on the street sometime before.

Heikki had seen the hat fly from the head of the victim and the boy nabbing it from the scene of the accident. It should have been handed over to the police, but Heikki didn't do that. He walked a block away from where the accident had occurred, carrying the hat carefully. It was dusty, and there was a fresh stain on it – blood, apparently – but that could be cleaned up.

Heikki shook strangely. He had a sudden urge to put the hat

on his head, but instead he tucked it under his arm and headed on foot toward the university. His research had reached the point where a breakthrough was near. He had formulated a mathematical equation that proved the existence of alternative realities. His professor had read his draft and smoked several pipes before admitting there might be some validity to Heikki's calculations. The professor himself was an expert in artificial intelligence and led a research group developing practical applications for devices that could repair themselves. The majority of the people out on the street didn't understand a lick of their research, but luckily the university had supporters. The government felt the research was important for keeping Finland on the cutting edge of development.

The further Heikki walked, the stranger he felt. Actually, he should have been conveying the bad news to the man's family. After all, that's what had happened when the hat had flown from the poor man's head: someone had lost a loved one. But to whom should he take the news?

Heikki slowed his step and came to a stop in the middle of the street. Ah, yes, Viljakainen's dress shop, of course. That's where he had been headed. He took a few unsteady steps in the opposite direction. He made his way past the people thronging the street and was nearly run over by a bicycle.

The two-storey yellow building was already visible in the distance. A hedge of hawthorns grew on either side of the gate. As Heikki whisked into the courtyard, his thoughts were laboured and viscous – he needed to come up with the right thing to say. A dignified message that would hurt as little as possible, if ever it were possible to soften the blow of such news.

The door opened, and at the gate stood a brisk, light-haired woman.

At that moment, Heikki's mind was wiped of everything. The words came from his mouth as if on a factory conveyor belt.

"This belongs to you," Heikki said, offering the hat to the woman, who took it in bewilderment.

Siiri

Siiri watched the gentleman leave the yard. It was as if this had happened to her before. The man and the hat. Siiri turned the top hat over in her hand and wondered what to do with the damn thing. It obviously wasn't hers. On the contrary, it would suit someone like Veerti. Maybe she could give the hat to her brother as a gift. It would look fine on him. Siiri went back inside. Mrs. Viljakainen was still in her dressing robe.

"Who was that?" she asked.

"I don't know. Some gentleman. He brought this. Does it belong to some outfit?"

Mrs. Viljakainen humphed. "I only make hats for women. That kind of hat would be worn to a very formal party," she said. "Or some gentleman could wear it at a funeral."

Someone walked over Siiri's grave. What was the old woman thinking, talking about funerals on a beautiful morning like this?

"After breakfast you could go to the market for some fresh vegetables," Mrs. Viljakainen said. "I have guests coming this evening."

Siiri replied that she would do as her mistress wished. Mrs. Viljakainen hobbled to the breakfast table, and Siiri hurried to pour her coffee. The hat she left on the kitchen table.

Mrs. Viljakainen spread the morning paper in front of her and looked up over the top of her glasses as Siiri poured her coffee. "Beware of the bus," she said suddenly.

"Why should I beware of the bus?" Siiri asked.

"It will bring misfortune to your family."

Siiri trembled. Mrs. Viljakainen was very astute and occasionally made predictions for her customers. She had never before said anything to Siiri about her future. Now she spoke clearly about what she foresaw, and afterward turned back to her paper without explaining anything.

Siiri had often wondered what the woman based her predictions on. Did she see future events, or simply guess? Did impressions come to her in dreams, or did she have visions clear as day? Surely there was use for a skill like that, but it must be a burden, too. Siiri wouldn't have wanted it for herself.

When Siiri went back to the kitchen, the hat had fallen on the floor.

"Aren't you skittish," Siiri mumbled to herself as she bent to pick up the hat. It downright clung to her hand. She turned the brim in her fingers. Its edge seemed rather sharp. She straightened out the dent, spit on a scrap of cloth, and rubbed out the stain.

Suddenly she had the urge to try it on.

Siiri adjusted the top hat to fit over her hair and turned to look at her reflection in the mirror. The hat looked stylish, even if it wasn't designed for a lady. Siiri turned from side to side. If only she were to add a full-length gown, she could go to a dance.

Then it struck.

She saw herself taking the top hat to a hat shop, to a master hatter who had taken a German name. She saw herself walking out of the place. She saw Veerti walking brashly out of the same shop, carrying a heavy bag of money, ogling the women walking in the street, and stepping directly in front of a bus.

Siiri cried out and lifted the hat from her head.

Oh, what a nightmare!

It was impossible! But why had she seen such a terrible sight? What was it Mrs. Viljakainen had said? There are many things in the world that are difficult to understand, but they exist nonetheless, and one must fight against them.

Her heart dropped. Siiri breathed and calmed herself. Her premonition grew into a horrifying certainty. Something bad had happened to Veerti. Mrs. Viljakainen had warned about a bus, too.

Siiri grabbed her coat, picked up the hat, and rushed into the street.

Veerti

Veerti laughed. That hadn't been difficult, not even close. All he had needed to do was slip into the hatter's workshop, get the chest of drawers open, and nab the purse stuffed with money.

There were coins and bills in there enough that Veerti would live like a gentleman. He would have the money to rent himself and Siiri their own rooms in an apartment in the city. They could go away somewhere and rent a house. Siiri wouldn't have to coddle the gentry any longer – people would fawn over them, instead.

Passers-by had no idea what Veerti was carrying. He patted his pocket. The purse was pleasantly heavy and felt real when he touched it from time to time. Of course, it was possible that the foolish old man would check his chest and notice the money was gone. But it would take time before suspicion fell on Veerti, if it ever did. He had been careful, no one had seen him, and the cleaner was so earnest that she would hardly be able to connect Veerti to the theft.

Veerti paused in front of a restaurant. He could go put some grub beneath his ribs, and the pints should be filled to overflowing. He would invite his drinking pals. Now it would be Veerti's turn to buy the rounds.

Suddenly a woman appeared in front of Veerti with something dangling from her hand. Siiri. His sister's face was frozen in a stern expression. It was the look their mother used to give him when she caught him stealing turnips.

"Well, hello, sister –" Veerti said, but Siiri was upon him in an instant.

"What have you gone and done?" she asked.

"Now, don't get all worked up," he said, speculating feverishly as to how Siiri had discovered what he had been up to. Had Iiris gotten in touch with Siiri and spilled the beans?

"We're giving the money back," Siiri said determinedly. Somehow, she had found out – damn it!

Siiri's grip failed. A gust of wind pulled the hat from her hand and it flew far away. Siiri ran after it, but a strong blast of air pushed her back beside Veerti. Siiri's hand touched his. In the blink of an eye, Veerti saw himself racing after the hat, though he hadn't gone so far as to attempt it.

At the same moment they heard a bang and a screech,

followed by shouts.

"The boy ran out in front of it!" a woman shrieked. "He was after the hat and ran right out in front of it!"

Heikki

Heikki picked the top hat up from the ground and gently shook the dust off it. The hat had a dent and a dark stain, wherever they came from. The hat wasn't his; it had been carried along by that gust of wind. Heikki glanced around. All about him was commotion, and he finally realised that something had happened. Something significant. He had just been on his way to the university when a noise had roused him from the depths of mathematical contemplation.

"The rascal ran right in front of it," a woman said.

"No, he was pushed by the woman in the hat."

"Who pushed him?"

"Or ran into him, rather. That woman with the top hat, she stumbled and bumped into him."

Strange. Had the top hat fallen from some woman's head? In any case, people had gathered to stare in horror at the little boy's fate. A young life had been snuffed out, just like that. The papers had written about and warned of the dangers of new technology – the spread of automobiles and their rapid acceleration had been mentioned in particular. There was no returning to the old days, when a policeman had stood at every intersection, directing traffic.

Heikki could have sworn that the hat ordered him to put it on his head. In any case, he did what the hat wanted.

The world danced topsy-turvy before his eyes, Heikki became dizzy, and his sight grew dim. Then he was present again, in his own body, whole.

"Dad!" Oskari cried out next to him and tugged at his sleeve. "Let's go see!"

"What?" Heikki asked, shaking his head. It was suddenly hard to say what he had just been doing. And Oskari... the boy was here, when he should have been at home with a fever.

"Some woman ran right in front of a bus."

"Is that so," Heikki said, unsure of whether it was Monday or Tuesday. Oskari was already running into the crowd when Heikki snapped out of it and ran after his son. "Stop right there! It might be a horrible sight."

Oskari stopped in his tracks, disappointed, and grumbled to his father about how boring everything was.

Everyone around them were swarming like bees in a hive or like crows around the carcass of a dead animal.

And then Heikki knew what he had to do.

The hat needed to be returned to the master, its creator.

Master von Hermandorff

"What do you want now?" the master asked the hat. He pressed it to his ear and listened. The clock mechanism ticked away inside. The spring and spring guide, piston, cylinder and piston head. A superheater? How on Earth could there be a superheater inside the hat? And a small steam pistol? How advanced! All of these features would certainly have commercial value, should he choose to make the drawings and take them to the engineers at the factory. His invention could have all sorts of industrial applications!

But he didn't have the plans necessary for mass production, and he didn't plan to ever make them. Instead, he worked out what he had already built for the mechanism and where it would all fit, since the false bottom of the hat was extremely shallow. The master took his tweezers and peered under the false bottom. The parts were very small; he would have to get the stronger loupe. He couldn't let his hand shake at all while using the instruments.

He pressed the hat against his bald head, and his mind was immediately filled with information that he wasn't fully able to process. This time, the thief hadn't been run over by a car. Instead, a little boy had ended up losing his life. A boy who sometimes was the son of the university man who would later pick up the hat – and at other times was just a passer-by. Or had the curly-haired woman ended up in front of the bus? The master couldn't say.

The hat moved from variation to variation, always learning new things. It was like a bloodhound on a scent, traveling at will between time and place, weighing and evaluating.

Now the master knew what he had to do. He needed to tighten up the mechanism, improve the working of the pneumatic cylinder, find the paths between realities. The aether vortexes, of course. When they flowed in opposite directions and rubbed against each other at an angle, the friction they formed created possibilities. From every moment and choice, the aether drew on the potential of what hadn't happened. The mechanism ticking inside the hat took reign of that potential for its own use.

But what would the master do with all that? There were seven hats, and this latest was the most developed of the lot. The hat didn't yet know enough about people and their choices. It was striving with all its might to get back into the field, to learn and to grow. It wasn't ready yet, not perfect as it wished to be. There was still a ways to go before it could affect the fate of nations, war and peace, the rise and fall of governments.

There would need to be many more choices and corrections and new choices made before the mechanism would develop sufficiently. But, in the meantime, the master could make a few more hats, experiment, and tinker.

For a fleeting moment, he considered that his dreams had perhaps led him to create a monster, but the idea was smothered faster than he could say his name. Had it been a dream, after all? Hadn't the master himself desired to create something unique, something the university men could only dream of?

The master laughed. Someday he would make a cylinder hat for the Swedish king himself, maybe for the emperors of Russia and Germany, too, because he would be able to. Then everyone would respect him. He was sure of that.

Anne Leinonen (b. 1973) is a multiple-award-winning, author, tutor, and editor of Finnish science fiction and fantasy. Her short stories have been published in magazines and anthologies, and they have won several Atorox awards. Her science fiction novels, such as *Viivamaalari* (*The Line Painter*) and *Ilottomien ihmisten kylä* (*The Village*), have received considerable critical acclaim, as has the trilogy she wrote in collaboration with Eija Lappalainen, *Routasisarukset* (*The Frost Siblings*). In addition to writing YA and adult fiction, she has recently started to work on audio and television drama. Leinonen moves fluently between science fiction and fantasy. Her stories deal with the themes of otherness and unfamiliarity, as well as the problems between a community and the individual.

Augustine

J.S. Meresmaa

Translated by Christina Saarinen

1.

To Augustine's mind, Jacques Gaston's smile was too broad, and it lingered on his face for no apparent reason.

A few weeks ago, Uncle Bernard had fallen on the stairs and broken his ankle. The Whittock repair works had just signed a major maintenance agreement with the Giffard-Krebs Corporation, and her uncle, concerned with the extra workload, had hired additional help. Perhaps the job was reason enough for Gaston's smile, since he had graduated only a few months ago from the mechanic arts program at the Paris Institute of High Technology and unlike many young men his age had found gainful employment.

Augustine sighed and straightened the stack of plans for Giffard-Krebs's newest airship. She worked carefully and cautiously; her fingertips were already stinging from two papercuts.

Augustine dreamed of studying, too, and had once snuck away from her uncle to the centre of the city and visited the institute's satellite office. The office, noisy and stiflingly hot, was crammed into a stone building behind Sainte-Chapelle and the courthouse. With trembling hands, Augustine had perused the academic catalogues, course schedule, and the entrance exam eligibility criteria. Her age was no barrier; at fifteen she was old enough to meet the requirements of the law. She didn't dare bring the material back to her uncle's house, though. If Bernard heard that Augustine wanted to study mechanical engineering and millwrighting at the institute, he would speak of nothing else. She could already imagine the words that would stamp out her dreams: *They don't accept females, and even if they did, certainly not half-deaf ones. So that's how you plan to waste your inheritance – on an education that won't do you a bit of good! Why on Earth would anyone hire you? Every school and institute is spewing capable mechanics into the labour market now that machines have populated the roads, skies, and waterways.*

In her uncle's opinion, Augustine should be grateful that he allowed her to live under his roof, eat at his table, and earn her keep helping in the file room, where she organised plans and did other office work.

Augustine stuffed the plans into the filing cabinet, rolled down the cabinet door, and started when she noticed Jacques Gaston standing in the doorway. His knuckles were resting on the door frame, so it was possible the young man had knocked. Augustine hadn't heard.

"I didn't mean to startle you," Jacques said. The big freckles on his nose and cheeks made him look thirteen, but Augustine knew that Jacques was at least twenty-one. Herbert Gaston was an old friend of her uncle's, and Jacques was Herbert's youngest son. At first, Augustine had wondered why her uncle had hired an outsider to take his place – and a recent graduate, at that. Then she heard from Nancy, their housekeeper, that during his studies, Jacques had done an apprenticeship at Ridderton & Son, where the world's first steam-powered flying machine had been developed. Perhaps her uncle thought that Jacques, with his up-to-date knowledge and experience, would have a lot to contribute.

"It's okay," Augustine said. "Did you need something?"

Jacques let his eyes roam around the file room. The familiar smirk flashed in the corners of his mouth. "Not from here. I was looking for you."

Augustine rubbed at the loose skin of her paper cut. "What can I do for you?"

"Gertrude said you might know where your uncle keeps his private customer registry."

"How do you know about that?"

"Holmsten mentioned it in passing during our lunch break."

Augustine gazed at Jacques' brown hair, which curled naturally at the ends. He kept it long, and a strand was dangling over his forehead – to say nothing of his neck. Augustine would have liked to find out if his hair felt as soft as it looked. "I don't know. Bernard is careful with his personal papers."

Jacques stepped over the threshold. He leaned against a filing cabinet a few steps away from Augustine, who discretely turned her head so that her good ear was towards Jacques.

"I had a look at the new contracts last night," Jacques said. "I know the notary has already been through them, but I wanted to be familiar with them myself now that your uncle has entrusted me with so much responsibility for the Giffard-Kerbs project. I thought it would be useful to go through your uncle's own notes. It was such a struggle to get the maintenance agreement, with competition being as strong as it is these days. Gertrude thought so, too."

Augustine considered asking permission from Bernard, but even the thought of climbing the stairs up to her uncle's room, with its stench of sweat and morphine stupor, was so unpleasant that she decided to act on her own. And if even Gertrude had given him permission to use the registry, it couldn't be such a big secret. "All right. I'll bring it to your desk tomorrow morning."

Jacques raised his eyebrows. "Can't you get it any sooner than that?"

Augustine shook her head.

"Well, I suppose I'll have to make do without it until tomorrow, then." Jacques raised his hand to make a gentleman's farewell, which looked a bit ridiculous, since he wasn't wearing a hat. His smirk lit up his eyes. "Don't work yourself to exhaustion here, Augustine."

Augustine continued standing there for a moment after

Jacques was gone. Her cheeks burned at Jacques words – though whether he was praising her or teasing her, she couldn't be sure.

After dinner, the work in the office and hall slowed.

Augustine climbed the circular metal staircase up to the office, pulled a key from her pocket, and went in. She glanced at Gertrude's desk. The pens stood neatly in their holder, not a single slip of paper lay on the desk, and the cover had been pulled over the typewriter. Gertrude had left for the evening.

Augustine let out the breath out of her lungs and stepped briskly to the door of Bernard's office. Light filtered through the blinds covering the window looking onto the shop floor, revealing the outlines of the room's furniture. Augustine turned the brass doorknob and drew the odour of Bernard's room into her lungs. Jacques had been working for them for only a week, but already a new scent mingled with the reek of cigars and her uncle's cologne.

Augustine moved briskly. She closed the blinds, lit the desk lamp, stepped up to the beechwood cabinet where the cassettes were stored, and fished another smaller key out of her pocket. After dinner, her uncle had received his dose of morphine and fallen asleep as if at the snap of a finger, and Augustine, who had even as a child had learned to observe adults silently and unnoticed, had known where to find the keys. She raised the cabinet's sliding door, lifted the cigar boxes out of the way, and felt for the place where the cabinet's bottom could be removed. When she found the screw that jutted slightly from the surface of the cabinet, she knelt down and tugged gently. The shelf lifted like a lid and revealed a shallow recess in the base of the cabinet. The unmarked cardboard folder felt heavy in her hands.

Augustine set the folder down on the desk and untied the ribbon. Inside, she found a bundle of papers and, after paging through them for a moment, she realised the customer registry wasn't all the folder contained. Her heart raced. If her uncle found out, Augustine was in for more than just a lashing: she would need to find herself a new place to live. She glanced at the door and the silent hallway beyond. If she was going to do this, she would have to go for it now.

She set the customer register aside and started to look through the rest of the papers. Bank documents, promissory notes, official-looking stamps and seals. Then her eyes fell on a name that was hardly ever heard in this building: Augustine Eleonore Blaise. Her own name.

A muffled noise in the office made Augustine drop the paper back into the folder. In a panic she gathered the folder and the customer papers into her arms, put out the lamp, and hid behind the desk. She strained to listen with her good ear toward the door, but heard only her own quickened breathing.

A light went on in the hallway. The thought that Bernard had somehow foreseen her plans flashed through Augustine's mind – maybe her uncle hadn't been sleeping as soundly as she had thought. But then she came to her senses. There was no way her uncle could have made it up the office stairs in his cast. Perhaps Gertrude had forgotten something.

The office door opened. Augustine's heart pounded. She squeezed the papers against her chest and pulled her knees up under her chin. She closed her eyes. The insides of her lids turned red. Someone had turned on the ceiling light.

"Augustine?"

Augustine was so terrified that she didn't recognise the voice, at first.

"I see the hem of your dress, Augustine." Jacques's voice purred with amusement.

Augustine clambered to her feet. She clutched the folder against her chest, too timid to look at him.

"Why on Earth were you hiding?" Jacques placed his hat and top coat on the coatrack beside the door. The smell of the gentlemen's club – leather, smoke, and self-importance – billowed up around him. "Surely you aren't doing something forbidden?"

Even though Augustine was sure he was teasing her, she couldn't do anything to stop the flush of heat rising to her cheeks. "Uh, I wasn't —"

"Is that the registry?" Jacques nodded at the folder and took a step further into the room. He circled around the desk opposite Augustine and plopped into a chair, its springs squeaking. He swung the chair around to face her.

Augustine squeezed the folder more tightly. "What are you doing here so late?"

"Working, working. Isn't that why you're slaving away here, too?"

Augustine took a quick glance at the cassette cabinet gaping open in the corner of the room. The cigar boxes and the cover of the secret compartment were strewn on the floor in front of it. Jacques noticed where Augustine was looking. His smile broadened. "I wondered where your uncle kept his cigars."

The air in the room was stifling. Augustine pulled the customer registry from between the folder and her thumb and held it out to Jacques. "I promised this in the morning, but you can have it now."

Jacques took the bundle of papers and laid it on the table. He didn't take his gaze off Augustine. "I suspect there's more to you than your uncle would have us believe."

"I don't know about that." Augustine shifted her feet. The toes of her shoes were worn. "I'm clumsy, and I don't always hear what's said to me."

Jacques leaned back in his chair. Augustine couldn't bring herself to look at him, but she heard the back of the chair creak. "I heard there was an accident when you were a child that damaged your hearing in one ear."

"I don't recall," Augustine said. "I was young."

"Was it the same accident that killed your parents?"

Augustine stared at Jacques. His expression changed, and he said, "Forgive me! It's none of my business. I don't know why I asked." He stood up from his chair.

Augustine found it hard to breathe. She turned on her heel and fled from the office. It wasn't until she reached the circular stairs that she loosened her grip on the folder she had been clutching with both hands and steadied herself on the railing.

2.

The engine unit of the airship *Goliath*, the newest pride and joy of the Giffard-Krebs Corporation, was towed into the shop, accompanied by its convoy.

Augustine followed the action from the little window in the file room. The men's voices and the squeal of the tow's cables rang out in the high-ceilinged shop. Representatives of Giffard-Krebs, dressed in top hats and carrying handsomely carved walking sticks in their gloved hands, moved among the mechanics and shop assistants in their coveralls, navigating the uneven floor and avoiding the greasy machine parts lining the walkways. Jacques walked among them in his short jacket and less expensive hat. Augustine could see his broad smile as he explained their operation to the company bigwigs. Augustine thought back to the question Jacques had posed yesterday, which had struck her in a place more tender than any bruise. Before returning to her uncle's house, a two-story stone building next door to the workshop, she had hidden the folder in the spare parts room on the far side of the shop floor. If only she had remembered that she wouldn't have the opportunity to sneak back and recover the folder today. The new engine unit would keep the workers busy late into the night.

A loud clang shook the shop walls as the tow lowered the engine unit onto a cradle over the grease pit. Two young assistants rushed to secure the cradle locks. Augustine watched them work for a moment before turning with a sigh to the work waiting for her in the file room. If only she could be below, too. There had been articles about the *Goliath* in all the papers, and she would have liked to see its innovative technology up close.

Her chest was still clenched with disappointment at

lunchtime. The large clock in the shop began to strike, marking the beginning of the break. Augustine opened the large envelope that had most recently arrived from Giffard-Krebs and let the plans spill out onto the table where she would review and organise them.

Gertrude stepped into the room. "Don't you plan to stop for lunch at all, Augustine?" Her broad figure filled the doorway. Her hair, pulled high in a bun graced with a few gray wisps, brushed the top of the door frame.

Augustine didn't hear exactly what Gertrude said; her bad ear was towards the door. But she had developed the ability to skilfully read situations, expressions, and contexts, so she was able to wave her hand and say: "I'll eat the sandwich Nancy made me later. I want to have a look at these first."

"Bernard wouldn't see a good thing if it bit him in the nose," Gertrude said and left.

This time Augustine heard what she said. A warm feeling pushed aside her despair. Gertrude was the only person who knew about Augustine's dream to study at the institute. In fact, it was Gertrude who had told Augustine about the Paris Institute of High Technology. Gertrude had noticed her interest in engineering early on, but knew as well as Augustine the reality of the situation: Bernard Whittock wouldn't in a million years grant permission for Augustine to study a subject like that.

Jacques's rash question revived thoughts that had occupied many sleepless nights when Augustine was a child. She realised she was thinking about her father, who, at least according to what she had been told, had been a brilliant engineer. Bernard had never said much about Frederic, leading Augustine to the conclusion that her uncle had never approved of her parents' marriage. Nancy had confirmed as much: Bernard had hated Frederic. As for the reasons, Augustine could only guess. But perhaps she had inherited her own interest in machines from her father.

Augustine eyed the plans for Giffard-Krebs's latest

innovation. For a moment, she allowed herself to dwell on the beautiful lines of the engine unit and admired the precision with which the draftsman had captured the creation on paper. Then she drew a deep breath and returned her attention to the plans, checking that each attachment was in its place and correctly numbered. It would be disastrous if at some critical moment they were unable to locate an important diagram.

She was running through the checklist she used when reviewing documents when a shadow fell across the doorway.

She turned to find Jacques Gaston's eyes shining at her.

"Augustine, it worked!" He bounded into the room and took her hands in his own. Enthusiasm emanated from him like an entrancing aroma. Augustine blinked. "Mr Roudeaux and Mr Maxwell were extremely impressed with what they saw. They want me to participate in the early phases."

"Wh-what do you mean?"

Jacques smirked. "When they heard I was involved in research at Ridderton, they said they most definitely want to take advantage of my expertise and to have me along in the planning."

Augustine looked at Jacques. "Are you planning to leave the position my uncle gave you?" She pulled her hands away. His touch had made her skin tingle, almost to the point of numbness.

Jacques tossed his hat on top of the filing cabinet and ran his fingers through his hair. "Lord, of course not! If your uncle has any sense, he'll do what I've been laying the groundwork for: The Giffard-Krebs companies have been growing like crazy these past few years, and they want their own maintenance division."

Augustine's mouth fell open. "So you're saying my uncle should sell us to Giffard-Krebs?"

"It would be a smart move in these times." Jacques had grown serious. He sat down on the corner of the table, and Augustine hurried to pull the plans out from under him. Her throat tightened. "Whittock is a relatively small repair shop, and, based on what I've seen, it's one of the best at what it does. But Bernard hasn't invested enough in updating the equipment or the shop. Giffard-Krebs would offer new workshops and top of the line equipment."

"I – I can't believe my uncle would agree to sell," Augustine stammered.

Jacques's smile wasn't as confident as usual. "Well, Augustine, sometimes there aren't any alternatives."

Augustine didn't care one bit for the bright, cold fire hiding in the young man's eyes.

3.

The shop floor was full of shadows when Augustine crept along the hallway from the spare parts room with the folder under her arm. After dinner, eaten in the kitchen with Nancy, the hours had crawled by, but Augustine had wanted to be sure that the mechanics had left for home before she retrieved the folder from its hiding place. Jacques's confidence that her uncle would sell them to Giffard-Krebs troubled Augustine so much that she had climbed the stairs and cracked opened her uncle's door. In the fading light that filtered in through the half-opened curtains, Augustine had made out the shape of her uncle resting in bed, his plastered leg propped up on a pillow. The sharp smell of cigars and morphine hung in the air. She didn't dare go further than the threshold. Even though Bernard Whittock had never had anything good to say about her, Augustine felt afraid and uncertain thinking of a future that suddenly didn't include the familiar office and filing and Nancy's sandwiches. Despite her lack of education and encouragement, Augustine wasn't stupid. She knew that if they were sold to Giffard-Krebs and her uncle made good money in the deal, Augustine would be the first one tipped off the wagon. Yesterday, while reading the legal and bank papers in her uncle's private folder, she had discovered that the only reason he tolerated her at all was because of the inheritance left by Frederic and Rebeca. When Augustine turned twenty-one, a portion of her inheritance would be split off, which would more than cover the money her uncle had spent raising her to that point.

Augustine's fingers felt damp against the cardboard of the folder. The beat of the hands on the large copper clock on the far wall were a dull ticking to her ears. There must have been a full moon that night, because a cold light streamed through the skylight, illuminating the silhouettes of machine parts awaiting service and the hard gleam of metal. The engine unit of the *Goliath* loomed on the central line like the back of a massive beetle. The shadows of the cranes' hoist chains were spidery legs cast onto the walls. Augustine turned to the right, toward the central line. On her way in, she had been too nervous to stop and admire the engine unit, but now she was sure that there was no one in the shop with her. She stepped carefully between the tools and spare parts lying on the floor and peered into it from the side, where a maintenance hatch had been left open. Thanks to the plans, she knew where the levers, pistons, and springs would be located. The engine unit smelled like machine grease and fresh metal. The exhaust pipes extended like wings behind the car.

Augustine gathered her courage, laid the folder on the ground, and climbed inside the hatch.

She had just pulled her skirt into the car and tugged free a wisp of hair from where it had caught on the head of a screw when a sound nearby made her freeze.

"Damn it! Pierre oughta be here himself to clean up his mess."

"What're you gonna do?" another voice said caustically. "He's got a needy wife at home, and an even needier brat in diapers." The smell of tobacco wafted to Augustine's nose. She could make out movement among the light and shadows. The men were close by.

Augustine heard a prolonged grumble. "The kid had to get the damn pox now. If he'd waited 'til tomorrow, Pierre could've explained his problem to the morning shift himself."

"Eh, quit your complaining. We hadn't got any further than the pub, anyway. You look over there. I'll have a look over here."

Augustine saw the glowering end of a cigarette and the shape of the man behind it. She pressed her back against the shell of the engine unit, hardly daring to breathe.

"Bloody hell! If his wife'd feed him better, we wouldn't be crawling around here because he's slimmed down so much he can't keep a ring on his finger."

Augustine heard a chortle of laughter.

"Too bad the shop's gas is cut off for the night. Otherwise we'd be able to get some more light in here."

"We'll see if Whittock's so tight-fisted when Giffard-Krebs fills his chest with coins enough to jingle."

"There's no cure for stinginess." Augustine heard the clank of tools being moved around.

"There's the truth. That new cockerel, though – he's different. He seems to understand that you have to give something to get something."

"I can't understand why old Whittock put that kid in as foreman."

"Didn't have much choice. Apparently Whittock is up to his eyebrows in debt to Gaston's old man. Hold up, what's this folder?"

Augustine's heart skipped a beat.

"Not Pierre's, that's for sure. Some maintenance files, probably."

"Well, we can't leave those lying around. Listen, we aren't gonna find that damn ring in this light. What do you want to bet Pierre didn't even lose it here? Let's leave a note for the morning shift so they can keep an eye out for it."

The other man yawned loudly. "Gotta admit I'm ready for some shut-eye."

When Augustine was sure that the men were gone, she climbed out of the car with trembling arms and legs.

Bernard's folder was gone.

In the morning, Augustine checked every possible place the workmen might have left it. She didn't find it among the incoming or outgoing internal mail, on the table in the break room, or even in the dressing room, from which she returned with cheeks ablaze. Finally, she shuffled up the metal stairs to the office and stood in front of Gertrude's desk. The lack of sleep was heavy in her limbs.

Gertrude raised her eyes from the page being spat out of the typewriter, and the dance of her fingers over the keyboard paused.

"Augustine, is something wrong?"

Augustine twisted the fabric of her skirt between her fingers. She had no choice but to admit everything, and Gertrude was the only person she could even consider going to.

"I lost my uncle's folder."

"Which folder?"

"The one he keeps in the secret compartment under his cigar boxes."

Gertrude was completely motionless for a moment. "The one with his private customer list?"

"Yes, but Mr Gaston has the list. He asked for it two days ago. But everything else. . ."

Gertrude stood up. Augustine's eyes stayed on Gertrude's face, which had turned pale. She felt her lower lip begin to tremble and tried to take a deep breath.

"Does Jacques Gaston have Bernard's customer list?" Gertrude asked.

"He needed it so he could prepare for the meeting with the representatives from Giffard-Krebs. I thought you knew about it." Augustine began to panic, though now for a different reason. "Sh-should I not have given it to him?"

The expression on Gertrude's face softened. "It's all right, dear. You couldn't have known."

"Known what?"

Gertrude cleared a few loose papers from her desk and collected her handbag and wide-brimmed hat from the coat tree. "I need to speak with your uncle."

"Am I in trouble?"

Gertrude stopped with her hand on the door frame. Augustine didn't meet her gaze. "Not you, Augustine. But someone else is."

4.

"You lied."

Sitting in her uncle's chair, Jacques Gaston turned to look at Augustine standing at the door. His shirtsleeves were rolled up and he had loosened his tie. He laid down the pen he had been tapping against his palm. His eyebrows raised at Augustine's words.

"You said you had Gertrude's permission to see my uncle's customer list."

"When would I have ever claimed something like that? You must have misheard."

Augustine's hands clenched into fists. It was hot in the office. The sunlight pouring in the windows that looked onto the shop was blindingly bright. "Two days ago. I want it back." Augustine reached out her hand.

Jacques pulled open a drawer and slapped the bundle of papers down on the corner of his desk. "Take it. I don't need it any longer."

Augustine pressed her lips together. She snatched the pile and retreated to the doorway squeezing the papers against her chest. "If my uncle had known you were a liar, he would never have hired you – debt or no."

Jacques's eyes brightened, and he straightened his back. A small smile spread across his lips. "So you know about your uncle's debt to my father?" He let out a little click of his tongue. "Augustine, Augustine. As I said earlier, you're a clever girl."

"My hearing may be poor, but there's nothing wrong with my head."

"I've noticed." Jacques leaned forward and placed his elbows on the table. "So surely you're aware that your uncle's debts were also behind your parents' fatal accident?"

"More lies."

"Do you think so?" Jacques pushed his chair back from the desk and stood up. "Augustine." He came towards her with hands outstretched.

"Don't come any closer."

Jacques paused and lifted his hands to calm her. "I'm only saying you should know all sides of the story before you start throwing around accusations."

She looked at the freckles on his young face, and at his eyes, which sparkled despite the fact that his expression was otherwise serious. She had been charmed by him. That was why her sense of betrayal was so strong that she dared speak so bluntly. But now she wasn't as sure. "Mother and Father were hit by a train trying to save me. It was an accident."

Jacques nodded. "An accident, doubtless. But you hadn't wandered onto the tracks, Augustine. Your family was waiting for a train at Gare du Nord and Bernard Whittock was there with you. Bernard's creditors targeted the wrong man, and when Frederic was pushed in front of the oncoming train, your mother tried to save him."

A blur of tears arose before Augustine's eyes. "That's not true," she whispered. "You can't know that."

"There were several witnesses, but only two of them understood what had really happened: Bernard and my father."

Augustine shook her head. "My hearing was damaged when I struck my head on the rails. I'm the reason my father and mother are dead. No one else, do you hear?" Augustine's voice rose. "Especially not my uncle and his stupid debts!"

"Augustine –"

Nancy was standing beside the stove making tea when Augustine burst in.

"Good Lord," she said. "First Gertrude and now you. Both of you look as if you've been caught out in a storm!" Then she noticed the tears streaming down Augustine's face. "Augustine?"

"Tell me, is it true?" Augustine sniffled and wiped her tears on her sleeve. She had barely been able to see in front of her when she had stumbled out of the machine shop, leaving her uncle's important documents behind in the office. "Tell me, am I an orphan because my uncle couldn't manage his money?"

Nancy stared at her with eyes wide. "But where is this –?"

"I hate him! Hate him!"

Augustine flew out of the kitchen and ran up the stairs. She passed the closed door of her uncle's room, pushed her own door open, and started to pull her clothing and other belongings onto the bed. She searched for the pitifully small suitcase that was a carryover from her childhood. The bag had languished unused since she had moved into her uncle's house. Now Augustine packed it so full that she struggled to make the buckles meet the straps. Tears rolled down her cheeks, and from time to time she paused to wipe them with her wet sleeve. She didn't want to cry, didn't want to shed a single tear on account of her uncle, but it was impossible to contain her disappointment.

She hadn't heard anyone come in, but a hand on her shoulder told her she was no longer alone. Gertrude. From the faint smell of cigars, Augustine knew that she had come from her uncle's room. Augustine shook off her hand. She caught a glimpse of Nancy in the doorway.

"Augustine, where do you intend to go?" Gertrude asked.

"Away." She checked the buckles of her suitcase.

"It's dangerous in the streets, dear. Your uncle will worry."

Augustine turned to look at Gertrude. "He's not concerned about anything other than maybe not getting his piece of my inheritance when I turn twenty-one in six years." Gertrude didn't look surprised. Augustine's stomach turned. "But apparently you're already aware of that."

"Perhaps it's best you have a seat and calm down."

"And did you know that my uncle is a murderer, too?" Augustine was so full of rage that she didn't know where to direct it all. "He let me believe that what happened to my parents was my fault. Can you believe it? He couldn't even take responsibility for that. And now he's planning to sell us to Giffard-Krebs!"

Gertrude took Augustine by the arm. Her grip squeezed like a vice. "He plans to do what?"

"That, dear Gus, is not correct."

Her uncle stood in the doorway, leaning on a crutch.

"That's what Jacques Gaston said," Augustine said defensively.

"Young Gaston says whatever benefits him most at any given moment."

Bernard Whittock's eyes were bright with morphine, and his skin looked doughy and lifeless. A pair of wrinkled pyjamas hung off him, and his robe was only slightly less wrinkled. Nancy stood behind him, looking as if she would have liked to remind him that, according to doctor's orders, he shouldn't be using a crutch, not until he'd received permission.

"What is Augustine talking about, Bernard?" Gertrude asked.

"The Giffard-Krebs companies would like to buy our skills and expertise. It's nothing new, but when we secured the maintenance contract the matter became timely again." Bernard hobbled on his crutch toward the armchair, and Nancy helped him sit down. She left the room.

"I'm your secretary, Bernard." Gertrude's voice was strained. "Why haven't I heard of this – or even seen the papers?"

"Because the few documents relating to the matter were drawn up in the gentlemen's club," Bernard said.

Augustine listened to the exchange. Her tears had dried up, but anger still coiled under her breastbone. She fingered the handle of her suitcase.

"Is that so?" Gertrude said.

Nancy returned to the room, carrying a footstool. She placed it in front of Bernard's chair, and he carefully lifted his plastered ankle to rest on it. Then his gaze turned to Augustine. "I heard what you said about your parents, Gus. I'm terribly sorry you had to find out this way."

Augustine swallowed. "S-so you admit it was your fault?"

"It was an accident."

"But it happened because you were in debt?"

Her uncle's lips grew narrow. "My economic situation was admittedly unstable at the time."

"And how about now? You're in debt to Gaston. Th-that's why you hired Jacques."

Augustine felt Gertrude and Nancy staring at her. She straightened her posture. "And that's why I believe that you intend to sell the repair shop and all the skills that we've acquired. You got Jacques to arrange the sale, and he'll take a cut of the money to cover what you owe the Gastons."

Bernard shook his head. "Gus, Gus. You have far too much free time if you're coming up with stories like that. You must have heard something wrong."

Augustine's face grew flushed. "I'm not deaf. And don't call me Gus. It's a stupid boy name."

Her uncle's eyes bulged. "Watch your tongue, girl!"

"Bernard —" Gertrude said.

"If you're going to be insubordinate, you can take a walk!" Bernard pounded the armrest with his fist. "Ungrateful klutz."

Augustine dragged her suitcase from the bed and showed it to her uncle. "See here, uncle. I've already packed. It would be interesting to know how you think you'll get your money from my inheritance if the law office isn't able to prove I've turned twenty-one."

She marched past Gertrude and Nancy and out of the room.

5.

She had to find out what had happened to the folder and the important papers it contained.

She scurried down the stone steps to her uncle's small front yard and ran to the gate that opened onto the street. The evening shift would be arriving soon. Maybe she could find the men who had searched for their friend Pierre's ring yesterday and ask them what had happened to the folder. If she intended to get by on her own, she would need the official papers her uncle had kept hidden from her.

But in the entrance to the machine hall she bumped into Jacques.

"Ah, so here you are, Augustine! Where are you off to in such a hurry?" Judging by his top coat, impeccable tie, and brushed hat, Jacques was going out. A black leather briefcase hung from his hand.

"Nowhere." Augustine wasn't prepared with a better answer.

"Why the suitcase?"

"I'm moving out."

"At the age of fifteen?"

Augustine lifted her chin. "I'll manage."

Jacques narrowed his eyes. His grip on Augustine's arm changed. "Come with me." He guided Augustine out.

Augustine looked back in alarm at the shop, where the workmen were bustling and the engine unit glowed in the sun. "Wait a minute, I can't..." She took a better grip on her suitcase, which was nearly slipping out of her hand. "I don't even have a respectable hat -"

"Who needs a hat," Jacques said and pushed her into a steam car waiting at the curb, its engine pounding and hissing. Black smoke poured out the exhaust pipe in its roof. While Augustine got a hold of herself and her skirt, which had tangled around her ankles, Jacques circled around to the other side, climbed into the vehicle, and pressed a switch in the ceiling. In the front seat, the driver placed his hands on the control levers. The vehicle shuddered into motion. Augustine clutched her suitcase in her lap.

"Where are we going?" She looked around in amazement at the steam car, which had been promoted in all the papers. Giffard-Krebs had invented this, too. It was the first time Augustine had travelled in one.

"I'm having a late lunch with Mr. Roudeaux."

The steam car jerked forward along the uneven streets. Augustine watched the endless rows of houses and factories through the round window, in the upper part of which there was a hinge attached to a lever that allowed the window to be opened for fresh air. She turned the lever. The window opened without a sound.

Black smoke poured into the vehicle and Augustine started to cough. Jacques reached across to crank the window closed again. The cool scent of him dispelled the black stench. "It's better to wait until we're further from the factories. The draft brings it all in."

"There should be propellers on the outside to direct the smoke away. Or a different kind of air circulation system could be built in," Augustine said.

Jacques watched her thoughtfully, amused.

The steam car climbed to the top of a small hill. The imposing church steeples and factory smokestacks loomed before Augustine's eyes. The airships puttering in the sky glittered like coins in the sunlight. A dark grey cloud hung over the densest colonnade of smokestacks at the city's centre. Augustine nearly pressed her nose to the window. She had hardly ever had the chance to visit the heart of the city.

"Breathtaking, isn't it?" Jacques said.

Augustine didn't answer.

The driver stopped the steam car in front of a stone building with wide stairs. Jacques climbed out and came to open Augustine's door. Augustine cast a puzzled look in the driver's direction. "Isn't he supposed to open the door?"

Jacques smirked. "The driver is part of the machinery. Literally. Giffard-Krebs is at the forefront of automaton design. This one here is being test driven."

Augustine would have liked to examine the driver more closely, but Jacques pressed her onward. "Otherwise we'll be later than fashion allows."

The foyer of Giffard-Krebs's headquarters was all handsome

marble and cold copper. A large scale model of the *Goliath* hung from the ceiling. Quiet voices and the clop of shoes echoed from the walls. The dampened clamour bothered Augustine: in that soundscape, she would hardly be able to make out what was said to her.

They were received eagerly by a boy dressed in a double-breasted jacket and meticulously pressed trousers who led them several storeys up the wide staircase until they were level with the model of the *Goliath*. From there they advanced down a hallway lined with thick wooden doors carved with images of cogs. The boy stopped in front of one of the doors and pressed a brass button in a decorative panel. The door opened inward, and they stepped into a reception area carpeted with an immaculate oriental rug. The clamorous echoes were left behind in the hallway. A spectacled woman stood up from behind a secretary's desk and stepped toward them. Augustine could make out violin music; based on the subtle rasping, it was being played from a gramophone disc.

"Mr Roudeaux will see you in a moment."

They sat on a wooden bench to wait. Jacques didn't say anything to Augustine, but she noticed he was nervous. Instead of a smile, the corner of his left eye twitched, and his fingers reworked his tie repeatedly.

The double doors at the other end of the reception area opened, and a thickly moustachioed man, whom Augustine recognised from the day the *Goliath*'s engine unit arrived, gestured for them to enter. A watch chain and a silver cigar case peeked from the chest pocket of his pinstripe vest. The man's mouth was turned up in a smile, but his grey eyes were sharp.

"Jacques! Come in!"

The windows of Mr Roudeaux's office looked out on the skyline of the city, which was dominated by the Scientist's Obelisk reaching up to the sky. The Seine was a silver ribbon flashing into view between the occasional belch of smoke from the factories.

Augustine tried not to stare. This must be what the world looks like from an airship. She shifted her attention from the view out the window to the dome-shaped lamp hanging from the ceiling. Brass appendages protruded from it, like the legs of an insect. Augustine shuddered to imagine such a large creature. Mr Roudeaux must have interesting taste.

Their host stepped behind his massive desk, drew the cigar case out of his pocket, and asked them to have a seat. Leather armchairs had been arranged facing the desk. When Augustine sat down, she sank uncomfortably into the depths of the chair.

"I see you've brought Miss Blaise along," Mr Roudeaux said to Jacques as he cut the end of his cigar. "Are the papers ready to be signed?"

Jacques reached into in his briefcase. "The notary went through them yesterday." Jacques pulled out the papers, freshly stamped by the notary, and laid them on the desk in front of Mr Roudeaux.

Roudeaux's cheeks puffed as he drew on his cigar and glanced at the papers. Soon the dark smell of the room intensified. "Excellent, Jacques." He reached to take a pen from a jade stand and offered it to Augustine. "If you please, Miss Blaise."

Augustine looked at the pen in astonishment, then at Jacques. "My signature? What document is this?"

Jacques fumbled with his tie again. "You see, my friend, the thing is, the Whittock repair shop isn't Bernard's lifework. The company originally belonged to your mother, Rebeca. Bernard merely worked there. When your mother died, the repair shop was transferred to your name, but since you were a minor and Bernard was your only kin, he kept the company running."

Augustine looked at Jacques in surprise. "How exactly do you know all this?"

Jacques cracked open his briefcase again and took out the folder Augustine knew only too well. Bernard's folder.

"This was waiting on my desk this morning. I've had plenty

of time to review the documents it contains. You're fifteen years old, so your signature is all that's needed on the bill of sale. If we'd known earlier, we could have saved a lot of time and trouble."

"So, the Whittock repair shop belonged to my mother?"

"Yes."

Augustine jumped to her feet. "I don't intend to sell."

Jacques tipped his head and looked at her like a child. "But Augustine, you don't have any choice. Your uncle's debts."

"Let my uncle handle his debts honourably himself, not dishonourably through others." Augustine snatched the folder from Jacques's hand, picked up her suitcase, and nodded briefly at the men. "He's a grown man, after all. Goodbye."

"Just a moment, Miss Blaise."

"Augustine, wait."

Augustine refused to listen. She marched to the door and yanked at the handle. The door didn't budge.

6.

"Open the door, please."

When nothing happened, Augustine turned around.

Jacques had risen to his feet and Mr Roudeaux stared at Augustine, the cigar forgotten between his fingers.

"Miss Blaise," Mr Roudeaux said, "I'm asking you to please sit down."

Augustine shook her head. She felt her palms begin to sweat. There was a buzzing in her ears. "I don't plan to sell my mother's property. It's too much to ask."

"I knew Frederic Blaise," Mr Roudeaux said, remembering at last to shake the ash from his cigar, which had gone out. "And your mother, Rebeca. Terrible accident, that thing with that train."

Augustine pressed the folder more firmly to her chest. "I'm asking you to open the door."

"Frederic was a talented engineer," Roudeaux went on. "His

inventions have benefitted Giffard-Krebs, as well."

Jacques threw a quick glance at Mr Roudeaux. Augustine didn't fail to notice. "Our automated steam car wouldn't be on the road without your father's superturbine. Here at Giffard-Krebs we appreciate innovation, and we encourage progress." Mr Roudeaux leaned his cigar against an ashtray and started to come closer. The man's face was friendly, but his eyes revealed that he was alert. "So I can assure you, Miss Blaise, that under our wing, the Whittock repair shop will be protected from the turbulence of the competitive market, and that, above all, we will respect its history."

Augustine shifted her feet. The mention of her father had opened a gaping hole, thirsty for more information. "I don't know."

"Think about it," Mr Roudeaux suggested, pausing next to the armchair where Augustine had been sitting. "The sale has clearly come as a surprise to you. I had expected Mr Gaston to have prepared you for it. We can certainly wait a day or two."

"No."

Augustine turned to look at Jacques, who had dropped his briefcase on the floor. The pistol in Jacques's hand was aimed at Mr Roudeaux. His mouth twisted into a one-sided sneer. "The deal will be done today."

The finger squeezing the trigger turned white.

Augustine cried out in fear. Her grip on the suitcase failed.

The reason for her outburst was not the weapon in Jacques's hand, but rather the mechanical creature that came to life on the ceiling. By no means was it an ostentatious lamp, as Augustine had assumed. The spider it had brought to mind was more accurate, because the brass appendages dropped swiftly down, striking the pistol from Jacques's hand. The weapon thudded to the thick carpet only a few feet from Augustine's shoes.

Mr Roudeaux laughed at Jacques's surprise. "Splendid, splendid! Arachne worked exactly as planned. It isn't often that its optic eye and reflexes are subjected to so authentic a test!"

"What...? How...?" Jacques stared at his empty hand. Then his eyes turned to focus on the weapon lying in front of Augustine. "Augustine! Kick it here!"

Augustine leaned against the door and silently shook her head. The contraption that Mr Roudeaux had called Arachne started to produce a strange squealing noise. Augustine heard it in the lull between the thumping of her heart. She stared in turn at the weapon and at Arachne.

Jacques lunged toward her, and suddenly Augustine had to make a choice.

She picked up the pistol and aimed it at Jacques, who stopped in his tracks. The weapon was surprisingly heavy, and Augustine needed two hands to hold it. She trembled.

"Don't come any closer! Stay where you are."

Jacques raised his hands. Mr Roudeaux was still standing next to the chair with his head cocked, like a spectator watching a performance. Arachne squealed and hummed, and Augustine had an idea.

"Augustine, give me the gun," Jacques pleaded. "I promise I won't hurt you. Put your name on the paper and we'll both be free."

Augustine stared into the young man's face. It seemed as if his freckles were going pale. His forehead gleamed and a thick vein pulsated on the side of his neck. "But I am free, Mr Gaston." Augustine engaged the safety and slowly lowered her hands. Jacques wrinkled his brow. Augustine exchanged glances with Mr Roudeaux.

He nodded.

From one of its many appendages, Arachne began to spew a dark rope – like spider silk, Augustine thought. The metal limbs wove a web with astonishing speed. Jacques turned to look in the direction of the noise.

"Our design department has done brilliant work." Mr Roudeaux puffed up his chest. "Now that progress has brought wealth to so many accounts, it has been necessary to diversify our security measures."

"What –?" In the blink of an eye, Arachne had thrown its sticky web over Jacques. He tried to shake free, but the more he struggled the tighter the black web grew.

"Nature is a treasure trove for inventors," Mr Roudeaux said. "You flounder in vain, young Gaston. No one escapes from Arachne's net." Roudeaux stepped towards Augustine. "Miss Blaise, please give me the gun."

Augustine pried her gaze from Jacques's reddened face and handed the weapon to Roudeaux. Her voice shook.

"W-would you open the door now, Mr Roudeaux?"

Mr Roudeaux's secretary guided Augustine into the reception area.

She was grateful to reach the cool air, where the clicking and humming of Arachne couldn't be heard. Her knees felt weak, and she sat down on the bench where just half an hour earlier she had sat with Jacques.

"Would you like a cup of tea, my dear?" the secretary asked, and Augustine nodded. She wanted to collect her thoughts. Jacques' flushed face arose again in her mind. The knowledge that she had the power to decide what would happen to the repair shop. Mr Roudeaux had known her parents. Augustine pushed her hair behind her ear. The secretary took a long look at her from behind her desk. The spoon clinked against the teacup.

The office door opened. Mr Roudeaux stepped into the reception area, but there was no sign of Jacques. Augustine saw Mr Roudeaux gesture to his secretary not to hurry with the tea. Then he sat beside Augustine on the bench. Augustine felt the bench sag under his weight.

"Gaston asked me to convey his apologies. He had to go out the back way," Mr Roudeaux said. Augustine's astonishment must have shown on her face, because he added, "There's an emergency exit from my office. He hopes you won't think badly of him. Apparently, he had a significant debt himself, and the noose was beginning to tighten. Gaston's life depended on the deal between Giffard-Krebs and Whittock being settled before the middle of the month. Gaston's father had promised him good money for the deal."

Augustine stared at her knuckles, which shone white where she had clenched them into fists. Her heart felt as heavy as a rock against her ribs. "He wasn't at all what I thought he was."

Mr Roudeaux patted her kindly on the knee. "We're all hiding something. Sometimes something good, sometimes something bad. I understand from your uncle that you're interested in studying mechanical engineering."

Augustine's head jerked up. "M-my uncle? He knows? How?" Then she realised. Gertrude. She must have told Bernard.

Mr Roudeaux's smile slanted his moustache. "You're rich, Augustine, but your wealth is tied up in property you don't want to sell. You won't receive your cash inheritance for another six years. That's a long time to put off your studies." Roudeaux leaned forward. Augustine met his gaze, grey and serious. Trustworthy.

"Perhaps we can reach some sort of an agreement. What do you think?"

Augustine sighed. "It's always about money."

Roudeaux's whiskers shook again. "Not always, dear child, but usually."

J.S. Meresmaa (b. 1983) is an author and editor of speculative fiction for all audiences. Her latest work is a steampunk YA novella trilogy Ursiini (The Ursine Affair) which is set in an alternate history Finland at the beginning of the 20th century. It combines science fiction and local history to form a thought-provoking, tightly-packed tale of the struggles of a minority in a world full of enemies – and a continuous threat of Russian mammoth army. The first part *Naakkamestari* (*The Jackdaw Master*) won a competition run by Robustos Publishing. The second part *Hämäränsäteet* (*Twilight Rays*) will be out in May 2018.

Her work has been nominated for Anni Polva Award, Kuvastaja Award, and Atorox Award. Her backlist includes a six-part epic fantasy series Mifonki, and a fantasy novella trilogy Keskilinnan ritarit (The Knights of Midcastle). She has also written over 20 short stories published in anthologies and magazines, some of which have been translated into English, Spanish, Swedish, and French. Meresmaa is a founding member of Osuuskumma Publishing.

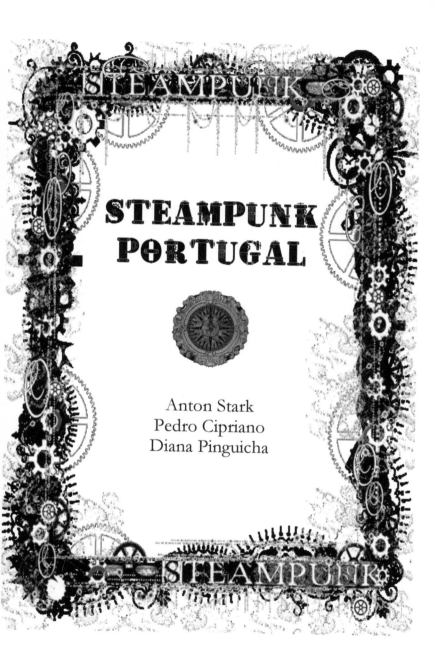

STEAMPUNK PORTUGAL

Anton Stark
Pedro Cipriano
Diana Pinguicha

Editorial Divergencia

Editorial Divergência is a Portuguese small press specialising in speculative fiction. Founded in 2013, it works mainly with Portuguese authors and creates limited editions and small print runs, with a focus on the quality of the finished book, and promoting an honest relationship with both its writers and readers. Editorial Divergência has organised the annual literary award Prémio Divergência – now renamed Prémio António de Macedo, as homage to a great Portuguese speculative fiction filmmaker and writer – aimed at promoting outstanding manuscripts written by new and upcoming authors. Divergência has organised several anthologies and published more than 40 authors. Two of its books have won the Choice of Year Award at Forum Fantástico, the national Portuguese SF&F convention.

Foreword

Pedro Cipriano

In 2011, Clockwork Portugal kicked off the first meetings related to the genre and, in 2012, they organized the first EuroSteamCon in Portugal. To accompany the event they produced the *Steampunk Almanac*, which brought together the literary and graphic sides of the genre. It was impossible, at the time, to write about Portuguese Steampunk without referring to the short-lived publisher Editorial Arauto, as it published *Prelúdio*, the first Portuguese Steampunk novel. This first Portuguese foray into Steampunk sparked several manifestations, including theme bars (such as Arranca-Corações, in Lisbon), fashion (created by Elfic Wear), and *Lisboa no Ano 2000*, a Portuguese retro-futuristic anthology. Several EuroSteamCons and Almanacs later, the artistic movement has matured, and is now represented by two major associations: Liga Steampunk de Lisboa (Lisbon) and Corte do Norte (Porto). They participate in many cultural events across the country.

Anton Stark was the first Portuguese author to be invited to write for this anthology. A long-standing collaborator of Editorial Divergência, he is, among other things, a prolific short fiction writer, both in English and Portuguese, and the author of *Prelúdio*. In his story, "Videri Quam Esse", he mixed historical fantasy and a little bit of steampunk with the Portuguese Renaissance as a unique backdrop. It is 1513, and the rhinoceros brought to the Portuguese court from India dies. The animal, however, had been promised as a gift to the Pope. It is up to the king's chamberlain, Garcia de Resende, to find a solution.

Diana Pinguicha is a Portuguese Young Adult fiction writer.

She is known for helping authors improve their manuscripts and for giving advice on how to approach literary agents. She has given several writing workshops and taken part in panels at Portuguese SF&F events. In her story, "Heart of Stone", she mixes science fiction and steampunk, creating a page-turner which once more asks the question: 'What makes us human?'

Pedro Cipriano, founder of the publisher Editorial Divergência, contributed to the first *Steampunk Almanac* as author and co-organised the 2017 edition. He is a prolific author of short fiction, with works published in several anthologies. In 2017, his debut novel, *As Nuvens de Hamburgo* (*The Clouds of Hamburg*), won the Choice of the Year award at Fórum Fantástico, the annual Portuguese SF&F convention. In "The Desert Spider", he wrote a Steampunk short story set in an alternative Porto at the beginning of the 20th century, where Portugal's Northern Monarchy Uprising succeed. It features Ana, a young spy, whose mission is to steal top secret military secrets for the Republic of Lisbon.

Pedro Cipriano
Sintra, Portugal
April 2018

Videri Quam Esse

Anton Stark
Translated by Anton Stark

The note came wrapped inside a fig in his supper.
Come soon. I have found a way to beat God.
By the time the paper burnt to ash, he was long gone.

From Albrecht Dürer's Rhinocerus:

On the first of May in the year 1513 AD, the powerful King of Portugal brought such a living animal from India, called the rhinoceros. This is an accurate representation. It is the colour of a speckled tortoise, and is almost entirely covered with thick scales.

"It's dead, Your Majesty."

"What do you mean, it's dead?"

The Indian bowed again and shook his head, a gesture which frankly bothered Garcia no end. His Royal Majesty, King Manuel the First, by the Grace of God, King of Portugal and the Algarves of Either Side of the Sea in Africa, Lord of Guinea and of Conquest, Navigation, and Commerce of Ethiopia, Arabia, Persia and India, sank into his chair, looking annoyed.

"It is just so, Your Majesty. It is dead," the Indian repeated, and made the sign of the cross. He was still making it, with a fervour normally reserved for frenzied zealots, when the king shooed him away and a guard dragged him out. Garcia de Resende set down his pen, stared at the tapestry on the other side of the room, and waited. The king's fury showed in every angry step he took towards the window, where he could glare at the

147

walls of the menagerie below, and then back to the throne to sulk in silence. Garcia looked down at the work in front of him, a hefty stack of shipping reports. In the margins, he'd managed to scribble two fifths of a song before the Indian had burst in with the news. Not half bad work, if he did say so himself.

"I promised that beast to the Pope," the monarch finally grumbled. "And now *it's dead.*"

Garcia could empathise. Manuel was the richest prince in Christendom, Portugal the richest kingdom. Yet it would have been easier to gift the Pope a solid gold rhinoceros, made from the treasures of Africa by the best smiths of Rua do Ouro, than to bring a live one from one of the many faraway lands where the naus made port.

"Can we be sure, Your Majesty?"

Manuel scoffed. "You heard the man, didn't you? Unless death means something else entirely where he comes from, the bloody thing's gone. Even though I promised it. *To the Pope.*"

Garcia tidied the papers on the desk, knocking one side of the stack and then the other against the mahogany. He took care to remove the sheet containing his song from the pile. He had more need of it than the Chancery.

"Quite so, Your Majesty. And what Your Majesty has promised, Your Majesty must deliver."

"I can hardly fetch another one in time, can I?"

Garcia shook his head.

"There is no need, Your Majesty. We must make do with what we have."

Manuel raised a bushy eyebrow.

"Do you have an idea?"

"*Aut viam inveniam aut faciam*, Your Majesty. With Your permission, you shall have your rhinoceros ready to be sent to the Holy Father within the month."

"Do you have any ideas?" asked Bernardo, pouring the last dregs of the wine into Garcia's cup. The tavern overlooked the Tagus, bathed in dwindling sunlight.

"None whatsoever," said the chamberlain, draining the wine in a single gulp. "I thought you could lend me a hand with that."

Bernardo rapped his knuckles on the table. He was twenty years Garcia's junior, but he had a mind as keen as any in Christendom. Keener, in fact, since it didn't seem to be overly constrained by the Church's teachings. This had enabled him to train under Zacuto's tutelage, to read not only the Jewish genius' mathematical tables, but also the texts of the Kabbalah and treatises from the old Orient. He'd learnt the secrets of locomotion and physics from a prodigy in Italy, metalworking from the Helmschmids in Augsburg. Even Erasmus sent a letter or two his way, on occasion. It was enough knowledge in a single person's head to warrant Garcia's constant protection as chamberlain to His Majesty. If anyone could produce a rhinoceros out of thin air, Bernardo de Salvaterra was that person.

"You're asking me to *make* you a rhinoceros."

"Am I?"

"I can't breed one, I can't fetch one. I could have it stuffed, but you wouldn't need me for that."

"Quite right. I need you to unmake the rhino's death."

"What if it was God's will?"

Garcia shrugged.

"Remember the Bible. God is entitled to a little mistake every now and then."

Bernardo looked at the empty jug as if hoping for assistance. None was forthcoming.

"I mean, without seeing the thing..."

"You can see it whenever you wish. The sooner the better," Garcia said, and thought that the phrase would work marvellously into his song.

"But even if I could do something, it would be dangerous work. Blasphemous. Heretical."

"Not to worry. I have the king's ear..." Garcia said, mentally revising the second stanza. How did it go again?

"Not to mention the materials, of course, and the labour..."

149

"… and the king's purse as well."

Bernardo looked away towards the sunset. It was gold where he gazed, where the river met the sea.

"There's no point arguing with you, is there?"

Garcia smiled. "For a genius, you took your time to work that one out."

It is the size of an elephant but has shorter legs and is almost invulnerable. It has a strong pointed horn on the tip of its nose, which it sharpens on stones. It is the mortal enemy of the elephant. The elephant is afraid of the rhinoceros, for, when they meet, the rhinoceros charges with its head between its front legs and rips open the elephant's stomach, against which the elephant is unable to defend itself. The rhinoceros is so well-armed that the elephant cannot harm it. It is said that the rhinoceros is fast, impetuous and cunning.

It lay on its side, a mound of grey hide, grey flesh, grey bone, all stinking to the heavens above.

"It's quite the beast," Bernardo said.

"It was," said the Indian, Ocem, wiping away a tear.

"It *will be*," said Garcia, prodding the carcass distractedly with the tip of his boot. "Do you know what you need to do?"

Bernardo sat on his haunches. He ran a gentle hand on the rhino's horn.

"I do. My Italian master taught me how to mimic natural movement in a suit of armour, and I believe the principle can be extrapolated to suit our purposes. But you'll have to bring it to my workshop. In secret. I don't want any onlookers."

Ocem spoke quickly, beating Garcia to the punch.

"What are you going to do to him?" he demanded. "This is a sacred animal! It was a gift from my Sultan, Allah bless him. I will not allow you to defile it!"

Garcia crossed his arms in front of him.

"We are not going to defile it, you fool. We are going to bring your rhino back to life, so that it can be given to the Holy Father in Rome. Understand?"

This time, the Indian didn't shake his head. His look was ice, sharp as the tip of the dead animal's horn.

"I do not like this, Christian. That is unnatural. That is sorcery. What is dead must so remain. You will not lay a finger on this poor animal."

"You're forgetting yourself, Ocem."

"I am not. It was a gift from my Sultan to your King, Christian. You cannot touch it."

The chamberlain's eyes grew hard.

"I speak with the king's voice."

"No king is greater than Allah, and only he can breathe life into the world."

Garcia buried his face in his palm. This was getting them nowhere. With a nod, he had two guards drag the Indian away, kicking and screaming and cursing his name in foreign vowels. The chamberlain nodded, disappointed. This much shouting in the middle of the morning was making him forget his planned third stanza.

"I do believe that was uncalled for," said Bernardo.

"Might have been. But at least now we can work in some degree of peace and quiet," Garcia said, humming verses under his breath.

The ending to the song eluded him.

It eluded him because of Bernardo's secret requests and reports. So far, he'd asked for copper and iron and coal, two smiths, a tanner, three jewellers and a shoemaker. He'd requested access to certain books in the royal library – translations of the Ancients, particularly the Greeks – and a few tomes Garcia had to smuggle in himself for fear of the Bishopric. He'd requested gold, enough to get more than a few curious looks from the chancery office.

It eluded him because of the screams that came from the palace dungeons, loud enough that the jailors had petitioned the head jailor to petition the major-domo to petition the king's chamberlain to petition the king to have the prisoner muffled, moved, or put to death. Sometimes the cries woke him during the night. Sometimes when he woke up he noticed his wife sound asleep next to him, and he knew he wasn't really hearing them; they were in his head, and he was clutching his crucifix so hard it hurt.

It eluded him because of the king's impatience, exacerbated by the murmurings around court of the precious beast's demise, and the deadline, his own idiotic deadline, drawing closer with every passing hour.

It eluded him because maybe, just maybe, the whole thing hadn't been the best of ideas to begin with.

This rhinoceros is covered all around in plates of leather scale so thick as to be almost metal. It is said the Indian prizes its hide for armour and shield, for almost no weapon can dent or pierce the rhinoceros' skin.

"We have a problem."

Garcia could see that. He could see their problem scattered around the workshop in bits and pieces, being worked on by a motley crew of artisans under Bernardo's direction.

They'd taken apart the animal. It had been scooped out like a mussel, and where once there had been organs there was now a skeletal copper structure propped up on a platform, to which several metal plates were affixed. Some of them had been covered with the beast's hide, and looked every bit the real thing. Others were still bare, which spoilt the overall effect. All in all, little more than half of the beast had been reassembled, and the deadline was closing in fast. The tables were strewn with clockwork mechanisms, wheels and coils and things he didn't know the names of. The head, hanging from a winch in the ceiling, lorded over the workshop like a thurible in cathedral mass.

"Do tell," said Garcia as Bernardo guided him towards the back and then up, to a loft that housed the polymath's study. The clanging from workmen around them was almost deafening. Bernardo sat the chamberlain down in a chair cleared of books and papers, before collapsing onto a stool in the corner.

"We can reproduce the bones and joints," he said, pointing to diagrams lining the walls. "We can tack back skin, we can stuff the head, we can induce movement... but it has no animus. No soul. No creature can function autonomously without one."

"I thought you said your Italian master..."

"Induced movement. A set range of motions, repeated. That is all we can do. I tried everything," he pleaded, and Garcia believed him. "I scoured the old texts. I found this thing, by Hero of Alexandria, a ball of metal that generates movement when heated. It's brilliant, it works just fine. But even that is hopeless without a soul to guide the machine. It would be like having a puppet on strings and no-one to pull them. It would fool the Pope for all of ten minutes, if that, if prepared beforehand. So much for the king's ambitions then."

"A soul. I dread to ask, but is there a way of giving it one?"

"Not that I know of, no. Unless..."

"Unless...?"

Bernardo eyed the bookshelf next to them. Then he shook his head.

"The Indian was not half wrong, you know? Only God should breathe life where there is none."

Two days before the rhinoceros was due to be loaded onto a ship and sailed away to Rome, and still no news from Bernardo. Garcia's song had been suffering as a result – sheets of paper tossed into the fire, one after the other, filled with inanities and minute, scared handwriting. For a man who prided himself on serenity and steadfastness, he was letting the situation get the better of him.

So they'd have to deliver a simulacrum. The king would be even more furious, of course, and would probably have him moved down to the chancery or removed from court altogether, sent packing to his holdings in Évora in disgrace. Still, he'd live. He'd keep to his songs, he'd have Bernardo make him drawings and plans for a palace, and maybe by then the blasted Indian would've shouted himself to death. No reason to be anxious.

The note came wrapped inside a fig in his supper.

Come soon. I have found a way to beat God.

By the time the paper burnt to ash, he was long gone.

The workshop was deserted. Only Bernardo waited for him, like a spirit, holding a dirty glass lamp. In the gloom, the disassembled rhinoceros looked like something out of hell. He wondered what curses the Indian would spout if he could see the animal now.

The polymath guided him back to his study, bid him wait as he set the lamp on the table, reached for a shelf and pulled out a roll of parchment. It was an old thing, scarred and creased and dirty. Bernardo laid it out near the light, and both men pored over it. Latin, and from before Constantine had been given his sign at the Milvian Bridge. Garcia's breath frayed as he read on. When he reached the end, he could not resist but to make the sign of the cross – out of relief, more than anything.

"How much do you believe in God, after all?" Bernardo asked apprehensively.

Garcia folded the manuscript with care.

"Enough to know," he handed Bernardo the document, and in his head he could see the final stanza in perfect form, and he smiled, "that He rarely cares, but always provides."

The animal eats leaves and shoots and pieces of wood and coal for digestion, and its belly is warm like a great furnace. Smoke rises from its nostrils and it bellows like a bull. It has dark eyes, small and sullen, and intelligent as to be almost human. It is one of God's prodigies on Earth.

Nuremberg, 1515.

He scanned the assembled populace for Bernardo, but then remembered his friend was indisposed. He'd probably be so for quite a while.

It was something to be seen. The crowd gathered around the beasts – forty-two of them, including caged leopards and panthers and parrots and fine Indian mounts, and all the necessary accoutrements and keepers and feed – around the soldiers, around the musicians decked out in Indian silks, around the carts laden with treasures beyond count. The canopies above the procession, the solemn looks of the clergy with their crosses held high. The elephant, with a little Indian fellow on its back, laughing as he guided the beast along and parted the throng in fear.

By his suggestion, the embassy to the Eternal City would go by land, dazzling the peoples of Europe along the way. The rhinoceros, however, would travel by sea, with a cargo of silver treasure and spices, along the southern coast of Castile and then France and then Italy. The less the beast could be seen out in the open, the better.

The nau was docked in front of them, near where the new tower-fortress would be built to defend the entrance to the river. In the royal tribune, King Manuel, every bit the perfect prince, clad head to toe in gold and velvet, bade him approach with the wave of a hand.

"Well done, Resende."

"Thank you, Your Majesty."

"So the thing wasn't dead then?"

"It was ill, Your Majesty. Our airs did not agree with it. The problem required… a delicate approach."

Manuel laughed. It occurred to Garcia he'd rarely seen the monarch laugh. Perhaps it took what they'd done to please a king.

"I don't know what you did or how you did it, but the beast seems even livelier than before. Certainly more belligerent. The Holy Father will be most pleased."

"Indeed so, Your Majesty."

"I would like you to convey my personal greetings to His Holiness when you meet him." He'd managed to convince the king to appoint him secretary to the ambassador, Dom Tristão da Cunha. He had a mind to stay as far from Lisbon as possible, for a while. "You have done me a great service; it is you who should have that honour."

"Thank you again, Your Majesty."

"In a way, it's a relief to see the beast go. It is a marvel of God, but not worth the trouble it causes. Speaking of which, what happened to that idiot, Ocem? You did get him released, did you not?"

"Oh, worry not, Your Majesty," Garcia said. The beast was making its way up the planks. As it climbed onto the deck of the ship, it stared at the royal tribune, with a look Garcia could only describe as sad. Prodded by its handlers, it trudged unceremoniously forward – a slow, inevitable march. A fitting end to the song, he thought. "I think he's around here somewhere."

Anton Stark was the first Portuguese author to be invited to write for this anthology. A long-standing collaborator of Editorial Divergência, he is, among other things, a prolific short fiction writer, both in English and Portuguese, and the author of *Prelúdio*. In his story, "Videri Quam Esse", he mixes historical fantasy and a little bit of steampunk with the Portuguese Renaissance as a unique backdrop. It is 1513, and the rhinoceros brought to the Portuguese court from India dies. The animal, however, had been promised as a gift to the Pope. It is up to the king's chamberlain, Garcia de Resende, to find a solution.

Pedro Cipriano, born in 1986, is the founder of Editorial Divergência, the leading publisher of Portuguese speculative fiction. His short fiction has been published in several anthologies. In 2018, Pedro created the SF&F literary award António de Macedo, granted to one unpublished manuscript each year. In 2017, his debut novel *As Nuvens de Hamburgo (The Clouds of Hamburg)*, won the Choice of the Year award at Fórum Fantástico, the annual Portuguese SF&F convention. He has also contributed to many other projects, events and literary contests.

The Desert Spider

Pedro Cipriano

Translated by Ana Piedade and Pedro Cipriano

The foul smell of wine and piss invaded her nostrils. When Ana entered the tavern, the mechanical piano was just playing the last chords of a Bach's Sonata, half drowned out by men shouting while playing cards. Her parents loved Bach's music. Thinking of them reminded her of how mortified they would be if they could see her in these dark boyish clothes. But, they couldn't.

She looked around, scanning the faces for her contact. Most of them wore airman's goggles, dirty uniforms and unkept beards.

There was a brief silence. All eyes settled on her. She could guess what they were thinking – that it wasn't normal for a sixteen-year-old, well-behaved girl to be here. In one regard they were wrong: she wasn't well-behaved.

"Come over here, sweetie!" yelled a fifty-year-old captain with greasy hair.

Ana ignored him and walked forward. She had found what she was looking for: the Scar, running from chin to the left cheek. The owner looked like a middle-aged grunt. She knew the type, people who usually think more with their fists than with their brains. It was expected.

"Are you an admirer of Vivaldi?" Ana asked, standing in front of him.

He glanced at her and smiled.

"Only of his latter works."

She sat in the vacant chair, facing the door. He drank from his cup, spilling some drops of red wine on his coat.

"So, do they send little girls to do a grown man's job now?"

This little girl would kill you before you could drop your cup, Ana thought. She raised her eyebrows. "I would love to sit here and gossip, like the little girl that I am, but I have a grown man's job to do. Do you have it?"

He nodded but remained still. Ana suppressed the shiver that ran up her spine. She took a little wooden box from her breast pocket and placed it on the table with her hand over it. His eyes shone and his fingers reached for the prize. Ana was quicker, pulling it away from him.

"Do you know what happens to those who double-cross us?"

He hesitated. She knew that showing any inkling of fear would spoil everything.

"Very well" he conceded, taking a steel cylinder from his leather bag.

This sergeant of the 2nd Royal Air Corps would face a firing squad if anyone found out he had sold the papers inside the container. If she was caught with them, she would be hanged. Just like her parents.

She still remembered how her mother's neck broke. However, Ana would rather share the fate of her mother than her father's. His death had been slow. He had been in agony as his body twisted and kicked, and his face reddened. At last, he had gone still.

Ana hadn't been able to take her eyes from the pair of them.

As soon as the cylinder touched the table, Ana grabbed it and let the sergeant have the box. Two one-carat round stones, enough to buy a small village. How many men would kill or die for them? Maybe the same number who would die or live because of the secrets she had in her hand.

She opened the lid and recognised the coat of arms of the Northern Monarchy. This fool had the nerve to steal the originals. He would not live long enough to enjoy those diamonds, she suspected. He held one of the tiny minerals in his hand, observing it closely before using it to scratch the table.

Ana stood and strapped the cylinder onto her leg.

"You are such a beauty! Would you share a drink with me?"

She ignored him and made for the exit. The sergeant just went back to his cup. The greasy-haired captain was looking at his cards. No one else seemed to have noticed her. She knew it had been a critical step, although the worst was yet to come.

Once outside, she saw two figures crossing the paved street. They were coming in her direction. Ana recognized the royal blue uniforms, illuminated by the gas lamps. These were not ordinary Air Corp's soldiers. They were Military Police.

She froze for a moment. Her heart raced. At last, she forced herself to walk away. She realised that if they were after her, she was as good as dead. Ana knew she could dispatch them quickly with her wrist blade, but she was also aware that she would never make it out alive. She would die a traitor's death, just like her parents.

She hadn't been able to shed a single tear. She'd stood there motionless as they lowered the bodies. No one dared to approach her. She had been unable to take her eyes from the scene, aware that she would revisit those memories countless times before she drew her last breath. They had tried to convince her that she didn't need to witness it, but she'd made a point of doing so anyway. There was no choice. She should have gone home, but she had already made up her mind to never return there. One week later, she began her training.

The two officers entered the tavern, ignoring her. She was relieved, but not for long. She fought the urge to break into a run. If they arrested the sergeant, it would be a matter of minutes before they come after her. After they realised what was stolen, they would never let the matter rest.

Fortunately, the street was empty. She turned into the first alley she came across. Ana had to think fast. There were no safe houses in this part of the city. No one in their right mind would situate one in the middle of so many soldiers and government officials. Even if there were, the sooner the parcel was sent across the border the better. She had to leave the city as soon as possible.

In the next alley, the monstrous three-storey red-brick buildings left her uneasy. The street was narrow and she saw no way to hide. There weren't any lights. Either people were already sleeping, or they were at the nearest tavern. More importantly, no one seemed to be watching her. She had no idea how much time she had. These were poor men's houses; one of those flats could be a safe house. She had no clue which. After all, it was not her style to go into hiding. That's why she was the best.

Ana knew why she was chosen for this mission, even though she was rather thin and not very tall for her age. Her combat skills were very limited and relied solely on agility and speed. She had no way to face an armoured soldier nor could fire a weapon. She had tried both in training, and failed miserably. In fact, they'd been ready to toss her into the streets before she mastered the art of knife fighting. That's when they started to see her potential. They had also realised that if she dressed in a corset and a long skirt, she would have the perfect disguise. Apart from the fact she wouldn't be seen dead in such a thing.

At the end of the alley, Ana saw movement to the left. Steamcars, the latest fashion. She though these people were stupid for wasting coal like that in the middle of a war, but progress was the trend, and those people would rather starve than go back to horse drawn carriages.

Ana noticed that the buildings were less monochromatic there. They were also bigger. The facades had brighter colours, big sash windows and slate roofs. She needed to be more careful, as these people tend to stay up until late. A girl with heavy grey pants wasn't a common sight in this kind of neighbourhood.

A Steamcar approached from behind. The headlights cast her shadow onto the sidewalk. She held her breath and kept walking, fighting the urge to look. If they were searching for her, she was dead already. In any case, it was better not to draw their attention.

The rhythmic noise of pistons passed by and the driver ignored her. Four wheels and seats, painted in a shiny black. That was a civilian's car, nothing to be afraid of. Some of her colleagues could tell a car's type by its sounds, but they could never read people's faces as well as she did. Ana knew exactly when they were lying and, more importantly, when they were afraid.

She followed the car until she reached the main street. Ana recognized the place: she was close to the São João Theatre. It was not very late, the upper class were going from their suppers to the theatre. Exquisite fragrances emanated from the ladies' dresses. They all talked happily in their northern accent, discussing the upcoming performance.

Ana realised that if her parents were still alive she might well have been in this kind of a street going to the theatre just like these people. She would have her ribs crushed by a corset. She would be wearing a bertha neckline dress with countless embroideries over several layers of petticoats. She doubted she would actually be able to walk with that, it would probably weigh more than her equipment.

Ana walked against the flow of the crowd, in the direction of the Maria Pia bridge. It was the only way she could cross the Douro river at this hour without being detected. If she attempted to cross the Dom Luis I bridge, the police might stop her. On the other hand, the railway bridge ought to be deserted.

Finally, she left the swarm in the direction of the fog. For the first time that night, she looked over the shoulder. No uniforms in sight. She didn't expect the rogue sergeant to resist interrogation. Ana guessed they would be looking for her already.

Her stomach was complaining. She had skipped dinner and had no food with her because the essential equipment alone was burden enough. She took a scarf from her pack and covered her head. She put on her leather gloves, then she looked around and jumped over the fence onto the railway track. The fog reduced visibility to a few feet in any direction.

Ana had no idea what was inside the cylinder. It could be the secret blueprints of the latest airship or armoured car. It could be military plans. It could be information on forces and movements of troops. Maybe some brand-new type of weapon. The less she knew, the better.

Soon she arrived at the bridge. She hadn't seen any train and wished she had thought to check the timetables. Only she hadn't. In fact, after she had seen the military police, she had stopped following the plan. Otherwise she would have had dinner by then and would be preparing to sleep in the safe house.

The two tracks were not far apart. The moon was not shinning and there weren't any lights on the iron-cast bridge. This was a railway-only bridge. Despite being an agent, she would be in serious trouble if she was found here. She progressed carefully, as one false step would plunge her 150 feet to her death.

The steam engines were no longer slow, as they had been ten years ago. After the second steam revolution everything became more efficient and powerful. Steam-powered engines mined coal a lot faster, and that had a knock-on effect.

She heard it before she saw it, the black engine approaching from behind. Without thinking, she jumped across to the other line, landing on her feet but losing her balance for a moment. Righting herself, she realised her mistake: she had jumped into the line carrying the train. Bending her knees, she jumped backwards, as she had done countless times in the training. The cargo train rushed past while she was still in the air. She felt it was taking forever to land. If she had miscalculated, at least she wouldn't live long enough to regret the fact.

She landed hard, winding herself. Her back hit the tracks painfully enough to leave her stunned. Then she felt herself sliding. Struggling to stay conscious, forcing her body to respond, she rolled and grabbed the nearest iron bar. It was a close one, another moment and she would have met her end. With her left hand, she pulled herself back to the rail line.

She allowed herself a moment to lie still and recover her

breath. The damn cylinder was still strapped to her leg. The back pain hadn't gone away. She found it difficult to move even her toes, each attempt sending a shock up her spine to her neck.

Her parents never had a proper trial. Ana clenched her fist every time she remembered. She could not forget the uniform worn by the news bearer. Black coat with the insignia on the shoulder and lapel. It was all black, including the cap and the shoes. She could smell the cologne. She guessed it was someone from the intelligence services. He was, at best, 25 and looked rather uneasy. She stood in her doorway, waiting for news.

"Miss Sousa, I am here to inform you that your parents have been charged with treason. They will be hanged tomorrow at dawn."

She tried to feel sad or angry, but she felt only emptiness. An invasion of emptiness. The same thing she felt following her first kill. The poor cadet from the mechanised infantry tried to prevent her from leaving. He wasn't much older than her. The blade came from her wrist and, before he could do anything, she had stabbed him in the chest. He opened his mouth, half astonished and half trying to scream, but he was unable to produce any sound. He grabbed her arm and pushed it away. Ana let him remove the knife. The blood sputtered from the wound and they both stared at it, surprised. So much blood, turning the situation into a mess. He grunted and tried to staunch the flow. Ana aimed for the neck, yet he grabbed the blade with his bare hands, slicing his fingers to the bone. She used all her strength, cutting through until she reached the spine. By then, they were both covered in carmine muck. She kept looking at him. His eyes widened and then he collapsed like an empty suit of armour. When she removed the blade, he was dead.

She took a deep breath and rose slowly. Although the pain in her back was less intense, each step was a torture. At least she could walk. It would have been better to let herself fall from the bridge otherwise. She would never be taken alive.

Ana was able to leave the railway line before another train came. Her legs were not responding well, and she felt clumsy. Even jumping over the fence took much more time than expected. She needed to stop and rest, only she couldn't while still in the city. They were looking for her, she was sure of that. The clock was ticking.

This side of the Douro river was much calmer. Most of those living here were workers. After a few yards, she started to see the effects of the war. Several houses had been reduced to piles of rubble. It was a daunting sight in the mist. The Zeppelin bombing campaign was producing results. The conflict between the Northern Monarchy and the Portuguese Republic had been going on for five years, ever since the Northern King proclaimed himself the ruler and declared independence.

Ana had no idea what time it was. Some point in the middle of the night was not good enough. She navigated through the sea of red bricks until she found a church tower. The clock there told her it was almost one in the morning, so her time was running out. By morning, she wouldn't have any hope of escaping. Weariness was defeating her. Her mind remained sharp but her body was not cooperating. Every joint ached and every muscle was stiff. Despite the discomfort, she pressed forward.

She had met her superior four days earlier, in his office.

"Miss Sousa..."

The look she threw him was enough to stop him.

"I apologise, Miss Ana, I mean Desert Spider, I have got an assignment for you..."

She finally sat.

"This is not a regular one and you may refuse it, though I believe you are the only one who can make it out alive."

He knew how to draw her attention.

"We've already lost two of our best agents on this. Raul Teles, you have met him, right?"

The bastard was trying to play with her feelings. Of course

she knew Raul, he was one of her instructors. Yet she couldn't feel anything, and that upset her.

"I will do it" she confirmed.

While limping through the streets of Gaia, she started to regret that decision. How could she have been so arrogant to believe she could infiltrate the enemy's capital, steal top military secrets and escape? The first two tasks were easy, but a whole country was after her now and she was still at least thirty miles from the border. No chance of covering that tonight. She needed a Plan B or she would be hanged by dawn.

Then she saw the two policemen. They were just walking in her direction. Could her false papers pass close inspection? She had never faced two opponents at once before and had never fought in the middle of the street. Ana attempted to keep her step steady and continued in the same direction. Her heart was almost jumping out of her chest.

They crossed the street and came towards her. By reflex, she unlocked the wrist mechanism. She had a spare knife in her belt but she was sure she would never be able to draw it.

"Excuse me, miss, we need to speak with you," the tallest said.

She stopped and feigned surprise. Ana had no idea of the proper response in this situation. She smiled and clasped her hands in front of her lap.

"Good evening officer, how may I help you?"

"We need to check your identification" he said, standing in front of her.

His colleague, clearly of lower rank, stood to the side. Ana took the forged papers from her waist pocket and handed them over to be inspected.

"Miss Maria..."

"Silva" she completed.

His eyebrows rose and she understood her mistake, she had told him the wrong last name. There was only one solution. She activated the wrist mechanism.

The first slash caught them by surprise. The officer threw his hands to his neck, trying to contain the blood from his slit throat. She attacked the other man the same way, only to strike metal as he lifted a defensive hand. He must have had arm protection. His other hand searched for his gun. Ana attempted to hold his wrist but she was no match for him. He pushed her and she fell backwards. The first officer collapsed at the same time. The second man drew his gun but hesitated for a moment, distracted by his fallen comrade.

Ana drew the knife and threw it. The blow was feeble and the blade striking his shoulder but barely sticking. She extended her arm and grabbed his wrist. She got up and plunged the wrist blade through his plexus, striking upwards. He punched her in the face but she resisted. Then, she was flung away again. Blood cascaded from his chest. He pointed the gun at her and pulled the trigger. She felt nothing. And then he pulled again before dropping down dead.

When the deafening sound of the shots faded, Ana felt a sharp pain in her arm. She stood up. Her back was hurting even more and she her left eye was half closed. She picked up her papers, stuffed them in her pockets and turned into the nearest alley.

Only after she had walked several yards did she realise she had forgotten to reclaim the spare knife, while her wrist mechanism had jammed, leaving that blade exposed. She was hurting even more than before the encounter and knew the shots must have been heard. It could only be a matter of minutes before the town was swarming with police and maybe even the army. She was covered in blood, with a huge blade strapped to her arm. Anyone would be able to spot the spy from a mile away.

She broke into a run. The police sirens could already be heard.

Ana had also heard the sirens when they came to arrest her parents. They all heard them, but no one took any notice until the door was knocked down. They were having dinner. She remembered it well: veal with potatoes cooked in the coal oven. The smell of roasted meat still brought bitter-sweet memories. The officer in his bright blue uniform strode into the dining room.

"Mário Sousa and Sílvia Sousa, you are both under arrest for high treason."

The soldiers invaded the room and seized her mother's arms. Her father stood to face them. The official gave the signal and they surrounded him and took their staffs out. Mário tried to strike the nearest one. Before the punch connected, three blows landed on him. He was hit repeatedly until he fell.

She stopped by a wall. This house must have belonged to very rich people. Ana unbuttoned her jacket and threw it over. Then, she climbed up and slid down on the far side. She was out of breath and sat down on the ground, leaning against the wall. She rolled up her sleeve and unstrapped the blade. Her arm had a nasty cut and was bleeding heavily. Ana got up and hid the coat and the blade behind some bushes. They could be found easily enough, but she hoped they wouldn't be for several hours at least.

She heard barking in the distance but growing nearer. She started to run towards the house. She could sense the dogs coming closer. Halfway there, and she was out of breath with her legs refusing to cooperate. She was conscious that she had no weapons. These dogs might kill her. Ana looked over her shoulder. She couldn't see anything. She kept running.

The first bite was on her right calf, it tore through the fabric. The pain in the back was sharp. A German Sheppard appeared in front of her. Ana accelerated and jumped over the confused animal. She landed badly. Her legs stopped obeying her. She felt as if someone were cutting her in two. A few more steps and the dogs got her. She screamed. They surrounded her quickly. She kicked out but failed to connect. She realised she was a dozen yards from the house. They barked furiously and came nearer. Ana screamed with all her aching lungs.

After the soldiers left with her parents she stood in the dining room, shaking,. Her mother hadn't resist, it wasn't in her nature anyway. Her father went out unconscious, bleeding from the nose. There was no one else home. For the first time in her life, she was all by herself.

The first dog attacked. She swung the left arm protected with the metal armour and hit him. The beast howled and missed, but by then she had lost her balance. The second dog came from the opposite side and landed on her. She hit him in the head but it seemed not to hurt him. Ana screamed and hit him again, while protecting her face with the other hand. She felt the bites on her legs. She thought briefly about the cylinder.

"Prince, Brutus, sit!" a male voice yelled.

The dog stopped and sat on her.

"Rebel, Beauty, come here!"

And then, there was no more biting. She was surprised there were only four dogs, they had seemed like ten. Her legs and arms hurt. There were tears in her eyes.

"Help me, please," Ana cried.

The man came nearer. He pulled the dog by the collar and removed it from her. He was in his early forties and had a pistol pointed at her. Ana felt naked without her blades.

"My God, you are just a girl" he murmured, and seemed to relax.

He looked like he had just woken up, even though he has fully dressed in a butler's suit.

"Can you walk?"

Ana nodded and tried to stand. Her legs and arms were bleeding. Every movement hurt. When she stood, the man offered her his arm. He had put his gun away. It crossed her mind that she could try to snatch it. She abandoned the idea. She was badly injured and she wouldn't make it through the dogs a second time. After the first step, she realised her legs were shaking. While walking in the direction of the house, she felt stupid and worthless: she had been captured by a butler.

They entered the kitchen and he let her sit on a chair.

"They got you... miss..."

"Sílvia," she completed and immediately regretted it.

Using her mother's name was not very clever. On top of that, she had no papers for such an identity.

"What happened?" asked a middle aged woman, entering through an interior door.

"I found her on the garden. The dogs got her. She must have climbed the wall."

"Look at the poor thing! She is injured, I must take care of her. Fetch Márcia, will you?"

The butler left. Ana realised she was still crying.

"What happened to you?" the woman asked, observing her arms.

"I jumped over the wall and the dogs got me," Ana answered.

"Why would you do such thing?"

Ana felt a shiver running on her spine.

"There were two men..." she stammered.

"My God, did they do something to you?"

"One tried to grab my arm, so I started to run. They didn't come after me..." she looked down.

"They would have been foolish if they had. His Lordship's dogs are famous in town, he breeds the best German Shepherds. Come with me, I need to dress these wounds."

They met Márcia in the corridor. She was slightly older and wearing a nightgown. Márcia covered her mouth with her hand.

"You must undress, we need to treat the wounds," the woman ordered as soon as they arrived into the adjacent room.

They left and Ana did as she had been told. She was careful to hide her arm plate and the cylinder in the middle of the torn clothes. Even though she was in her underclothes she felt naked. Without her equipment, she was just a normal girl. She knew she had to take advantage of that.

The two women came back with a bowl of tepid water and towels. Ana thought Márcia was pretty. She had green eyes and dark, curly hair. She wouldn't be a servant forever. Ana realised that, unlike her, Márcia would marry well.

They made her lie down in the bed, washed her cuts and bites, and dressed them. She could feel every cut on her skin.

"Please, don't tell anyone..." Ana pleaded.

"Oh, dear, we must tell your family..." the woman answered.

"They don't know I was out, I went to meet a boy... Please, don't tell anyone!"

They looked at each other and Márcia nodded.

"We have to tell his Lordship. But we will make sure that no one else knows about your circumstances."

Ana didn't find that very reassuring. It was a long shot and she had to take her chances.

"Rest now, I will find you something to dress," Márcia promised.

As the maid left, Ana felt the tiredness take hold. She fought the exhaustion, but fell asleep.

Ana was back home. His father was tending the pigeons in the backyard. As a hobby, he bred them and had even won a few competitions. Ana watched him. He was a handsome man, despite having a few grey hairs. Ana was sure those hazel eyes were the reason why her mother had fallen in love with him. Mário filled the bowls with corn. Ana was unable to move. Her father closed the cages and faced her.

"Do you like them?" he asked.

Ana nodded.

"If anything should happen to me, would you take care of them?"

Ana woke up covered in sweat. Her first glance was towards her clothes. They were still in the same place. Her heart raced. She couldn't tell if the conversation with her father was a true memory or a dream. So much about her parents was fading away.

The door opened and Márcia came in.

"What time is it?" Ana asked.

Márcia put down some clothes on the edge of the bed.

"Half past four, you slept for about two hours."

"I need to go" Ana tried to get up.

"You will do no such thing, you are injured," Marcia answered, holding her shoulder. "A doctor will come in the morning to see you."

"I can't wait. I have to be home before my parents wake up or they will kill me!" She let one tear down her cheek.

"If that is what you want, then put this on and Mr. Alberto will see you out."

"Thank you," Ana muttered.

Once Márcia left, Ana strapped the cylinder and the armour to her legs, trying to avoid the cuts. Then she also tied her clothes in a bundle under the clean petticoat. The dress was plain beige with sleeves. She regretted having to leave her boots behind, but they would never fit in that outfit. She hid them under the bed and left.

Márcia, who gave her proper shoes. Ana smiled and put them on. Even without a corset, the strapped equipment and dress restrained her movements. It would be impossible to run, let alone to fight.

As the butler took her to the gate, the faint shades of darkness in the sky were receding. The sun would come up within the hour. The butler watched her closely, and Ana could tell he didn't trust her. She had to move fast, they would report her as soon as they found the blade.

Ana went limping in the direction of the railway. She had some money with her, so she went to the nearest bakery. She saw the policemen too late. They were standing by the counter when she entered. She realised she couldn't leave without raising suspicion. She felt her legs shaking as the other costumers looked at her.

"... if you hear anything about the spy, let us know. He is quite dangerous and has killed two policemen already."

The owner nodded.

"How could such a thing happen here?" one woman in black said.

The policemen left, and the gossip started. Ana felt the sweat on her forehead, and fought the urge to run away. If they realised who she was, she wouldn't make it to the exit. Her joints were stiff. Ana noticed that some people were still looking at her. They must have noticed she was not from their neighbourhood. She took a deep breath, and stared straight forward the whole time.

"What do you want?" asked the man serving, barely looking at her.

Ana pointed at one of the baskets behind the counter.

"One of those."

"Fifty reis."

She gave him the coins, took the bread, and left. Ana walked to the railway, being careful to avoid the street where she had killed the two policemen. She stopped only at the fountain to quench her thirst after eating the bread. When she arrived at the station, the sun was rising. Ana knew it was too late to sneak out of town. Her only hope was to hide in plain sight. She went to the counter and bought a ticket to Estarreja, the last station on this side of the border. Luckily, the clerk didn't raise his head from the desk.

Ana waited in the small station. She was surrounded by a crowd carrying baskets, bags and even live animals. The noise was terrible. Now and then, they felt the ground trembling as a mechanised armoured soldier patrolled the platform. She felt an itch on her left arm. There was a red spot on her sleeve. She rolled the fabric to find she was still bleeding. Ana adjusted the binding to delay the blood flow.

She heard the engine approaching, after which the train took only a few seconds to arrive. It came from Porto in the south. Ana boarded the 3rd class carriage like most of the people on the platform. All seats were taken and she had to stand. The train set off again as soon as the doors closed.

Outside, the landscape was changing: fewer and fewer buildings, and more open fields. The strapped equipment was hot against her legs, making them itchy. The red spot on her arm was growing. She rubbed her eyes, trying to keep them open. Some men threw dirty looks at her and she avoided eye contact.

The trip took hours because they stopped at every little village. It was lunchtime when she arrived to Estarreja. Ana wandered through the streets. She quenched her thirst in the fountain but had no money left to buy lunch.

She went to the outskirts. Away from the town's noise, she could hear the sound of cannons. The border was only a few miles away. Neither faction was attempting to advance; instead they opted for trench warfare. Ana had to cross the frontline to deliver the contents of the cylinder. But that would have to wait for nightfall.

Behind a wooden fence, she saw a hut-like structure stuffed with straw. It had potential to hide her until nightfall as it was almost full and the entrance was not pointing to the road. Ana jumped over the fence and crawled inside the tight opening. A few feet inside, she heard something crack. A sewer-like smell filled the cavity, causing her to gag. She had broken a rotten egg, forcing her to throw most of the floor's straw outside. In the end, she had no choice but to lie down on the bare earth.

She found out her parents were spies when she was fourteen. Ana couldn't recall the exact moment that happened. One day she overheard a conversation. Later she found an encrypted message on her father's desk. Then notes her mother made about newspaper articles. And the pigeons. It puzzled her why some of them didn't have rings.

Ana woke at sunset. Her arm was the first thing she felt. The sleeve was soaked red. Using the cover of the straw piles, she took her dress out and used slices of it to make a tourniquet. She dressed in her black uniform, put on the arm plate and strapped the cylinder to her leg. She hid the pretty clothes in the middle of the straw. She was hungry and thirsty, yet she waited for darkness to fall before she headed towards the trenches. Ana knew there were no good places to cross the border, so she just walked South.

Soon, she abandoned the road. The soil was wet and full of grass. Now and then, there were patches of mud. There were few bushes and fewer trees. Not much in the way of cover. The moon was almost at first quarter, giving little light. She walked as silently as she could. Soon her shoes were full of dirt.

Despite her caution, Ana almost stumbled on the last row of fortifications. Fortunately, they were nearly empty. She climbed down into the tunnel and went forward, knowing that she would have at least three miles to go. Each row of trenches was a thousand yards distant from the next, but only the first in the line was fully manned, these other two were used only as a fall-back, in case the enemy should breach the frontline. The bottom of the hole was full of mud and wooden logs were required to shore up the sides.

She heard the first sentry whistling before she saw him. He must be new, she thought. Ana hid in one the vaulted sections and waited. She had done this a few times before, though never without her blades. The sound was getting nearer, so she got ready to leap. Ana felt a stab of pain in the leg bitten by the dogs. She considered taking another approach because she was risking too much. But that was not the Desert Spider's style.

When the soldier passed by, she jumped him. They both fell. His gun landed a couple yards away. He was still surprised when she took his knife. He pushed Ana away, causing her to miss his neck by an inch.

"Be still or you die," she hissed.

His eyes widened. His beard was not yet fully developed.

"You are a girl" he stammered.

Ana got up, pointing the knife at him while she grabbed his gun.

"What do you want?"

"Your uniform." She smiled.

"They would kill you if they found out. They would kill me as well..."

"I can kill you now!"

Shaking, he took off his boots, his jacket, and his trousers.

"I need to tie you down, okay?"

He nodded and she motioned him to get inside the vaulted area. When he passed by, she slit his throat from behind. He reached for his neck, the blood flowing between his fingers. Ana pushed him inside. The soldier fell down. She waited until he stopped moving to drag him to a corner and cover him with some planks. Then, she undressed her dirty rags and put on the uniform. The boots were too large, but were still better than the wet lady shoes she had on. She hid the papers on the uniform's shirt. She left the gun with the body and took only the knife.

Ana crossed the last and the second row of trenches without seeing anyone. The walking was taxing her and the wound on her arm was bleeding more and more. She was sweating. Soon she heard voices. She guessed it must be sentries. Ana went to the right, attempting to avoid them. She climbed down at a corner, after looking both ways. She went forward at a brisk pace with eyes cast down.

Ana reached the frontline unchallenged. She just had to climb into no-man's land. Immediately, she crouched and moved very slow, taking as much cover as possible. She tried not to think about stray bullets. Soon, Ana reached the wire. She has no tools to cut it, so she went to the left until she found a join. She undid the tangled wire with her bare hands. The metal cut through the skin, but she didn't quit until the two pieces were separated.

She squeezed through the hole. She advanced from one shell crater to another. Her fingers were raw. The moon shone with wan light. No one could see more than a couple of yards ahead.

Suddenly, the sky turned green. She lay flat on the nearest

crater. She heard the artillery deliver their payload. Then, a salvo from the other side. More shots were exchanged. She felt a shock reverberate through her bones. One mortar shell landed nearby. It left a buzz in her ears. The green flare fell down and everything returned to darkness and silence.

Ana didn't waste any time. When she found another row of wire, she knew she was close. She did her best to separate the two halves, but her fingers were not able to complete the job. She tried to pass through but the jacket got stuck. Another flare went up, the green light again spreading over no-man's land. She ripped the fabric and got rid of her jacket, running the last yards in a crouch. One shot. She jumped into the trench, landing in the middle of a group of soldiers.

"Don't shoot! I'm on your side!" Ana yelled.

They pointed their weapons at her and looked to each other.

"It's a girl!" shouted one.

The soldiers searched her, removed the knife and then locked her in a bunker.

"Please tell Major Gomes da Silva from 4th Mechanised that the Desert Spider is back" she said before they closed the door.

When Ana read the content of the cyphered letter on her father's desk, there was only one thing to do. She reported them in the nearest police station.

The Major came at noon. When they opened the door, she was asleep.

"Here you are..." he said, sounding amazed but pleased.

Ana tried to get up, but fell back to the floor. She took out the papers.

"I *knew* you could do it!" he said, taking the documents. "You're in a bad shape. We have to get you to the hospital."

Major Gomes da Silva shouted a few commands and two soldiers appeared with a stretcher. As they were carrying her away, he smiled broadly and said, "Welcome home!"

Heart of Stone

Diana Pinguicha

Translated by Mário de Seabra Coelho

Alirvi tinkered with the controls embedded in titanium, the screen on her mechanical forearm shifting from static to camera feed. As she adjusted the imaging device hanging by an aetherian tether over the streets, the black-and-white image it captured reproduced on her arm. Gifts from her Mechanist allies, received after she survived the destruction of her mentor's lab – an act she'd come to avenge.

Thinking of how pissed the Evolutionists would be once they found their precious Sidallite gone, it was hard not to smile; Ali couldn't wait to witness their much-anticipated fall from grace.

"The guard patrols are changing shift soon," she said upon examining the image. "Barron, take point."

The soldier stepped from the shadows, goggles reflecting the lights of both the stars above and the firefly lamps below. He took the hook gun from the bag on his back and dropped into a prone position on the roof to take aim. "Ready on your mark."

Their team was to infiltrate the Church of Evolutionism, where the mineral they needed was secured behind thick steel walls and under heavy guard. They had studied the layout for days, devising their plan. Now, they stood at the cusp of its execution. The smoking chimneys had been their only way in, presenting one very smoldering challenge: the fires from the coal-burning process raging in their depths.

But Ali hadn't been Dr. Forel's student for no reason. She fingered the canisters on her belt, liquid nitrogen bombs she'd crafted last night. Throw a couple down the chimney and the ever-burning fires would die down. As for getting down...

"Gravity reversers?"

Behind her, the noise of tightening screws. "Charged and ready," Gail confirmed, patting the spherical heads with affection. Ali took one, hooked it to her belt. The Reverser was more familiar to Ali than the palm of her own hand – well, the palm of her right hand; her left was new, mechanical, and she hadn't got around to studying it thoroughly yet.

Eyes flitting to the screen on her arm, Ali resumed spying on the guards, already restless for the end of their shift. When their replacements arrived, the black-clad men huddled together to exchange reports. She summoned the imaging device and it flew to her hand, a bird made of a hard metal shell covered with disguising feathers. It chirruped when it landed on her arm, and although the bird was supposedly a machine, Ali couldn't help feeling affection as she scratched the top of its tiny head. The mechanical animal rewarded her with a nuzzle before it bent in on itself, turning into a cube which she stowed in her bag. She could almost swear she felt happiness emanating from the pocket she'd lodged her imaging device in, a kinship she rarely felt towards people.

Putting the fantasy of a machine with feelings out of her mind, she turned to Barron. "Now," Ali said.

From their vantage point atop the bell tower, the Mechanist Sergent shot the hook at one of the chimneys. He pulled the taut line and, at his nod, Ali hooked her wheel. Her wrist on the leather handle, she jumped off the roof and slid quickly along the cable. The impact of her legs on the metal chimney reverberated through her body, and when she grabbed onto the edge, her flesh spared the heat thanks to the thermal-isolating bath her leather clothes had been subjected to. She used her metal hand to hold on, and tossed two nitrogen bombs with the other.

The canisters clanked on their way down, followed by a hiss and a cloud of steam. The metal cooled, and Ali raised herself up to sit on the edge, signalling Gail and Barron to follow.

Lowering her goggles and putting on her breather, she looked down at the funnelling depths of the chimney, the vapour and darkness making it impossible to see the bottom. Taking a deep breath, Ali palmed the Gravity Reverser at her belt, and let herself fall.

One second.

Her stomach dropped out from under her.

Two.

Her shoulder bumped against the chimney.

Three.

Her feet scraped the wall.

Four.

Hands at her side, she righted herself.

Five.

The ground rose to meet her. Ali pressed the button on the reverser, the device coming to life in her hand. A force seemed to reach out from above, grabbing Ali before the fall claimed her life. Her insides flipped, her limbs jerked, but…

Looking down, she saw her feet hovering just above the ground. A hum played in her ears as the Gravity Reverser at her belt vibrated and wheezed, like a dying animal giving its last keen.

Ali dropped the rest of the way, feet sliding on the frozen coals as she went deeper into the now icy furnace. From the satchel at her side, she produced a vial filled with a fluorescent yellow liquid, so bright it was as though the sun shone from within, strapping its cord around her neck to cast away the darkness.

Gail and Barron joined her not long after, their liquid lights at their breast, and the other woman walked towards the door, portable blowtorch in hand. Sparks flew as the mechanic worked on the door, and both Ali and Barron used the time to look over the Vault's map.

"The Sidallite is five floors below ground," Barron noted, his voice distorted under the breather's influence. With his finger, he drew a line between where they stood, at basement level, and the mineral coffers. "Once Gail's through, we'll have little time before the Church send in a team to fix the furnace. As soon as they see the ice, they'll realise we've infiltrated them."

"We'll take the vents as planned. Here," Ali said, tapping the point in the map. "It'll take me a minute or so to open them, though, so we'll have to move fast."

Although Barron's goggles hid his eyes, she could feel them on her. "I hope you're as good as Forel claims."

She gave him a sideways glance. There wasn't a patrol she couldn't evade, nor room she couldn't get into. She had stolen the map Barron now bent over; she'd been the one to steal shift schedules, and the plans for Evolutionist weapons that had given the Mechanists a fighting chance against the dominating faction of their Technocracy; she'd been the one to tell them about the Sidallite, and how it was all they needed to end the mad Evolutionist rule.

"A bit late to question my capabilities, Sergent," she spat.

However, she'd be lying if she said she wasn't a little bit nervous, or that she did not doubt herself. After all, her first foray into robbery had ended when Dr. Forel caught her red-handed; the only reason Ali hadn't been left to rot in the Guarda's jail was because the old man had seen promise in her quick fingers and quicker wit.

Ali remembered it as clearly as if someone had captured the moment in rollfilm and played it behind her closed eyelids. The dirty streets of the city she called home, cobblestone roads, and the far-away noise of refineries and power plants a distant bustle; how the smell of oil had plagued her, and the sight of sparks seemed to follow her dreams; how her stomach growled when Dr. Forel walked past, the hem of his brown Mechanic uniform dragging along the mud. With his hunched shoulders and downcast eyes, Dr. Forel had looked to be an easy target, and no one had been more surprised than Ali when he'd caught her hand just as she relieved him of his money.

She recalled the panic, throat-numbing and heart-throbbing. She'd expected him to deliver her to the Guarda, where they'd chop off her offending hand. Luckily for her, Dr. Forel wasn't fond of the authorities, and had taken her to his workshop instead.

"I *could* take you to the authorities," he'd said. "But I'm in need of an apprentice with clever fingers."

It hadn't been a difficult choice. Despite the illegal nature of her job, Ali hadn't regretted it since. Forel often remarked that she learned things faster than previous apprentices, and he willingly fed Ali's aptitude for knowledge, frequently and in great quantity. Soon, the sight of machinery, the scent of oil and the heat of steam, had become her natural environment.

An environment the Church threatened with their insistence that humanity needed to use only what the Earth provided. As the dominating faction, they'd all but stamped the Mechanists out of the University, but had allowed the weaker group to remain active. As much as the Church despised machines, they still had need of them.

Back then, Dr. Forel had been developing limb replacements to help those who'd lost arms or legs to Mecha factories or hungry Evo creatures; but his ambitions grew to impossible heights. He'd begun speaking of creating a fully-sentient automaton using both natural and artificial materials. They'd been close to finishing the first prototype. All that stood between them and a breakthrough in science had been the Sidallite.

A conductive mineral like no other, Sidallite was a Church creation, obtained through a complex mutation process combining carbon and aether. Desperate, Dr. Forel had gone to the last Evolutionist he considered a friend, asking for a small sample to power the prototype.

But the Church viewed his newest pursuit as the utmost sacrilege. Machines weren't meant to think by themselves, and so, that very night, they'd sent a team to blow up Dr. Forel's lab along with the scientist himself.

Ali would've been blown up too, had it not been for her mentor. She remembered that, too, with incredible clarity: the scent of gunpowder hitting her nose, along with Forel's despaired scream to *jump*. How she'd fallen towards the river below, away from the deafening blast that sent glass, steel, and stone flying out above her. A flash of brightness and the impact on frigid water rattling her bones. The current, carrying her away in a furious embrace, remnants of Doctor Forel's laboratory peppering the river behind her.

Survival instinct tore through the haze and the pain. Ali struggled to get her limbs moving, to focus her cloudy sight. She kicked against the current, took in mouthfuls of water in her attempt to swim towards the rocks near the bank. She dreamed of sparks and oil, and woke up the next day in a Mechanist safehouse, Gail putting the final touches on Ali's new arm, saying they'd found her half-dead on the riverbank, her left forearm mangled beyond recognition by explosion and rocks.

Ali did not mourn the partial loss of a limb. It made no sense to do so, not when she had a metal one that was much better in almost every way. Not when her chest lay empty, the absence of the man who'd taught her all she knew a hole no other person could fill.

Ali looked down at the smooth titanium surface with tenderness. If she, Barron, and Gail succeeded, the Church would no longer control the world.

Barron grunted, and Ali had the feeling he meant to continue voicing his doubts, but the sound of Gail's blowtorch ceased, and the thick metal door slid open with a protracted creak. Silence stretched between them, then shattered when a deafening siren rang in every corner of the room.

"Malfunction on Boiler Three! Malfunction on Boiler Three!" someone announced through the speakers. "All personnel, please proceed to the nearest safe room."

Ali dashed to the nearest vent, hand falling to the loop on her belt where her custom screwdriver hung. She pressed the tool against the screws, and with a push of the button at the top, the metal end began to rotate, powered by the charged aether-stone within.

Thirty seconds later and all the screws were in her pocket; she dove into the tunnel with Barron behind her, Gail bringing up the rear. The metal walls echoed when the mechanic slapped the vent back into place, their home-cooked adhesive paste hissing upon touching the metal, sealing it together.

If the Church somehow figured out they'd come this way, at least they wouldn't be following any time soon.

Ali crawled forward into the smoke-filled vents, the path she'd memorised clear in her mind. A left turn in the first intersection, then straight on until the metal floor of the vents dropped into darkness. Using her hands and feet, she slowly made her way down.

The temperature increased with each downwards shimmy, the steel at her back turning warm to the touch. On the third floor down, the vents changed into stone, growing hotter the lower they went.

Ali's feet met solid ground. She stuck her upper body into the lowest vent, the sound of muted conversation echoing from somewhere ahead. At first, Ali ignored it, resuming her advance, but her hands almost slid out from under her when she heard her name, a distant ghostly whisper bouncing on the stone walls of the tunnel before her. She believed she'd imagined it, but then it came, again and again.

An intersection stood before her: on the left, the path to the Sidallite; on the right, the voices, saying *Alirvi* between other words she could not fully discern. Her gut roiled in unease, demanding she took a detour – just a small one, merely five minutes – to find out why her name was on the Evolutionists' lips.

Her mission too important to cast aside, Ali meant to take the former option – yet her name reached her ears once more and, before she could stop herself, she grabbed the ledge of the lower third floor vent and hauled herself inside.

Barron tapped at her ankle, and, from behind him, Gail asked, "Why did we stop?"

"No idea. Ali, get moving!" the Sergent hissed angrily.

"I overheard something that might be important," she said over her shoulder, taking the right path. "You two go on ahead. I'll meet you below."

Whatever Gail and Barron said after that fell on deaf ears as Ali crawled along the stone, her breather the one reason she hadn't choked on the hot air. Sweat beaded on her forehead and fell down her temples, catching on the straps of her goggles. The siren grew muffled, the voices became clearer, enough for her to make out everything they said.

"... sound ... Forel's secret to get the Alirvi to work?" a man asked.

What in the rust were they talking about? "It couldn't have been the Sidallite," another said. "We only found out how to use the aether to mutate ore years after he left us." A weighted pause. "Could it be that he never got the Alir to work? It could've been a lie meant to confuse –"

"He definitely got one to work. I saw it myself, sneaking around the Academia a couple months ago. The day the blueprints disappeared. It was far from perfect, but it was *alive*." A shake of the head. "Shame it blew up with Forel's laboratory. We could've studied it."

Her throat seized, rendering Ali unable to breathe. It was somewhere around two months ago that she'd broken into the Academia to steal the original blueprints of the Vault. Had this man truly seen her? And if so, why did he believe she was some sort of thing, nothing but a construct of Dr. Forel's?

At the grate, Ali took off her goggles to peer through one of the square holes carved on the stone. A dim environment lay on the other side, and from this angle, she could spy the white-robed Evolutionists, standing between two rows of six cylindrical tanks, their contents...

Ali gagged, but forced herself to remain still as she took in the aberrations floating in liquid. The view wasn't the best, the lack of light made it hard to see, and she could only see into four of the tanks – yet it was enough for her to be sure of what they were.

People, deformed in unfathomable ways. One, an adult man, with a beak in place of mouth and nose, arms that were feathery wings, and the feet of a bird; opposite him, an adult woman with a slumbering feline face, and giant, tiger-like paws for hands and feet; a child, no older than five, a mass of tentacles sprouting from his head; a young girl who looked to be made of stone. All of them had their eyes open, unseeing –

Their gaze suddenly shifted to her.

Blank, yet conscious. Unfeeling, yet desperate.

They made us from bits and pieces, tailored to their needs.
End us.
So many like us died, only to be improved.
We can't live outside.
Replaced.

Free us.
We can't stay here, forever watching their madness.
Please.

Voices, distinct, yet somehow alike, spoke into Ali's head. The four people from the tank, talking inside her head – but how?

What were the Evolutionists doing down here? What could possibly warrant these radical experiments? What did they tell themselves in order to sleep at night?

The man who'd been speaking put his hand against the curved glass. "She was too similar to this replica. Forel could've made his own Alir based on this one. That, or he got a Version I to wake up *and* survive."

Alir.

Version I.

Alir-vi.

She looked down at her hands, one of metal, the other flesh.

Though Ali longed to dismiss the scientists as deranged, doubt wormed its way into her thoughts. Could she truly be an artificial construct, brought to life in a tank and not a womb?

"Either way, we should get back to work." The man moved to a nearby table, his robes a white blur in his wake. "Where were we?"

The other scientist joined him, leaving Ali to debate whether to linger or to rejoin Barron and Gail. She'd already risked the plan by coming here –

A noise split the air, grating at her ears before its claws shredded its way into her brain. Her head seemed to explode, draining the strength from her body; whatever sound emanated from the Evolutionists' contraption worked its way into her bones, shattering them to pieces.

Slumped in the confined space, a scream tore past her lips before she could stop it, then another, and another, until her raw throat could produce nothing but a croak.

The infernal noise ceased, her body left shivering in its wake, muscles seizing, fingers spasming. Her wits began to gather, enough for Ali to realize she'd rusted up, and rusted up *royally*.

"It's the Alir. It's still alive," one of the scientists said. "The frequency must've done something to it…"

"I'll call backup."

"Go. I'll find where it's hiding."

The man's hand moved to the machine again. Not one to be caught off-guard twice, Ali dug into her satchel, instantly finding the rectangular bundle she needed. A twist and a yank, and she had her mufflers over her ears, blocking out all sound.

Though her legs trembled beneath her, Ali brought herself to a kneeling position between ragged breaths, a plan forming in her mind. Risky, but she had no other option. She screamed, this time on purpose, impatiently waiting for the scientist to approach the grating.

Using all the strength in her metal forearm, she punched; the first hit cracked the stone, and the scientist lost his balance from fright, falling backwards onto his behind; the second splintered the grating, sending bits flying towards the gasping white-robed man. She lunged forward, and her mechanical hand found the man's throat; his lips moved, but whatever sound they formed failed to get past her earmuffs.

Ali dragged him to the machine; without letting go, she kicked at the table's legs, the infernal device crashing to the ground. For good measure, she stomped it, crushing the body until the red light at the base went out. She uncovered a bit of her ear, and when she failed to pick up the brain-imploding, bone-crushing sound, she took the earmuffs off, stowing them haphazardly in her satchel.

"What. Are you. Doing. Here?" she asked, furiously. "What have you done to the people in the tanks?"

What have you done to me?

The man's lips opened and closed, making him look a clueless fish. "You... you're alive."

"No shit." A squeeze of her fingers, and she brought him closer, their noses almost touching. "I'll ask again, once. Just what. Exactly. Are you doing here?"

His face hardened. "My colleague went to get help. There's no hope —"

Ali shook him. "*Answer me!* What are you doing to these poor people?"

The man tightened his jaw; she was about to shake him again when he spoke, "They're not *people*. They're not even alive."

"They are," Ali hissed through clenched teeth. "They spoke to me. Whatever it is you're doing to them, they'd rather die."

Whatever reaction she was expecting, it wasn't wide-eyed wonder. "I was right. Forel really did succeed."

"Stop talking as if he made me; he didn't. He found me in the streets."

He blinked as if confused. "But he did make you." He lifted his arm, index finger jutting out towards the tank he and the other scientist had talked about. "He made you right here, shortly before deserting us and joining the Mechanists."

Ali's attention darted to where he pointed. The young girl floating in the transparent liquid stared back with eyes exactly like Ali's own: coal-black dotted with purple, a combination too rare to be coincidence.

Her breath left her, and she almost dropped the scientist. A hum arose at the nape of her neck, and a girl's voice said, *Sister.*

A gurgle; a soft crunch.

It was only when her arm sagged under the dead weight that Ali realised she'd killed the scientist. Part of her should have felt bad, but she could summon no pity. She let the body fall with a heavy thump, her feet already moving to the tank, as if of their own accord. At the bottom there was a label, which read:

Artificial Live Intelligence Replica
Version I

Oh, rust.

She placed her right hand on the glass. Staring at the girl was like looking into a mirror ten years ago.

Her sight blurred with tears. This was her, and not. A replica, made from the same mould Ali had been. A creature devised in a test tube, grown in a tank, birthed behind glass.

Sister, please, the girl whispered into Ali's head, at first alone, then joined by the others.

Please.

"Breach! Breach!" the same voice as before blared through the speakers. "All combat units to the Bio-Development Laboratory. Non-combatants, please proceed to the nearest safe room."

A turmoil broke inside Ali's head, setting her in motion. With one last look at her genetic sister, she punched the glass tank. Cracks splintered the glass, which then shattered; thick liquid rushed out, drenching the room with a sweet, fleshy scent and delivering the replica into Ali's waiting arms.

The girl gasped, suffocating on the air as though her lungs hadn't been programmed to draw breath – as though something as simple as *breathing* hadn't been coded into her genes. Ali's doppelganger shuddered as her skin turned blue, but not even the pain of death erased the smile from the girl's purple lips.

Laying the replica down, Ali turned to the other tanks, and the room soon flooded with transmuted bodies and the flesh-scented liquid. Like the girl, they died quickly, unable to breathe.

As she moved, it occurred to Ali that the scientist could have been lying, or mistaken; that Ali was the basis of the Version I replica, not an earlier incarnation of it. Otherwise, how come she was alive when this one had choked on its first breath?

Ali didn't have time to wonder. With two tanks left – the bird man and the feline woman – a squad of twelve soldiers burst into the room, the mouths of their guns pointed at her.

The one at the lead yelled, "Freeze!"

Ali considered the unwinnable odds. She could hide behind one of the two tanks, but the glass wouldn't last long against the bullets. As for weapons, she had a screwdriver in her belt, the liquid light dangling from her neck, and a spare nitrogen bomb in her satchel. They'd have to do.

If she was meant to die here, it would not be without a fight.

Before they could react, Ali jumped behind the bird man's tank. Bullets didn't take long to splinter the glass, which shattered the next moment.

More liquid whooshed forward, and she used the distraction to dive behind the precarious safety behind the feline woman's tank. She withdrew the last nitrogen bomb from her satchel, and waited for the perfect time to strike.

The soldiers' aim shifted. The tank collapsed, unleashing another wave of liquid. Ali jumped onto the nearest table and flung the nitrogen bomb at the squad's feet.

The thin shell broke, the white smoke rising from its carcass instantly creating a sheet that froze four squad members, killing them instantly. As the room chilled to impossible coldness, Ali slid along the ice, seizing the guards' momentary confusion to pass by the frozen bodies and break through the open door. She stabbed her screwdriver into the first neck she could reach, and held the screaming man up as blood spurted out, his body shielding her from the bullets flying her way.

When the soldiers paused to reload their two-shot pistols, Ali dropped the now dead man and moved towards the closest one still standing in the corridor; a hard kick broke his leg, and a shove of her screwdriver into his eye did the rest.

A sharp pain on her shoulder told her she'd taken too long; a bullet to her leg reaffirmed it. Ali picked up her latest victim's gun from the floor and shot one soldier in the head as another bullet ricocheted off her metal arm.

Her screwdriver found another eye just as a bullet hit her stomach. Pushing the pain aside, Ali yanked at the liquid light's necklace, breaking the vial open on a soldier's face. He screamed as his face melted, then collapsed into stillness.

Heaving, Ali took in the remaining three men, free from the ice that had held the others in place. Their guns fired in unison. She spun, desperate, but only managed to avoid one bullet, the two others piercing her chest, almost knocking her off-balance.

The screwdriver slipped on her bloody fingers, and her legs, both injured, threatened to give. Ali breathed deeply, forcing herself to focus.

The three guards came at her, guns either forgotten or out of ammo, and knives at the ready—looking to finish her off quickly. What was it with men ending conflicts with knife fights when it was easier to shoot? She'd never understand it, but she wasn't complaining.

Gripping her one makeshift weapon tightly, Ali side-stepped the first blow, then rolled away when her left knee buckled. She rose on one leg, the momentum helping her shove the screwdriver into the side of a man's neck.

She yanked it out, and her closed titanium fist found its target in the face of another guard. Bone crunched under her blow, and Ali barely had time to keep herself from falling when a blade pierced her chest –

And stopped.

As stunned as she was, the guard grunted, pushing harder. Blood flowed as it scratched at her ribcage, ripping a scream from Ali's throat, and yet...

The blade didn't – wouldn't – go any further in. The scent of oil reached her nose, black liquid mingling with the red. With a twist of her metal hand, she snapped the man's wrist, took the knife from her chest and plunged it into his. He crumpled to the floor, as lifeless as the replicas they'd condemned to the briefest of existences.

Ali slumped to the ground and, with her back to the corridor's wall, took inventory of her injuries. Two bullets in her left leg, one in her right thigh. One in her right shoulder. Three in her torso, a couple somewhere in her back – more than she'd realised during the fight.

Her eyes started to close, her thoughts began to fade. Yet what shook her the most wasn't her impending death, but the fact oil oozed from her body instead of blood. A funny buzz built in her chest, travelled into her bones; it felt as though her entire self had become a trembling malfunction.

Ali no longer had any doubt: she *was* a replica, one Forel had done something to – something the Evolutionists would never do under their doctrine. It was why she'd lived when the ones around her had died.

She coughed into her hand, spitting out more oil. Her limbs fell into spasms as her consciousness faded.

Forel's deceit shredded her heart, but what did it matter? Artificial person or not, she was going to die here today.

"Rusting hell, Ali!" Gail's voice reached her muzzily.

It took all her remaining energy to open her eyes and turn her head to face the mechanic. "How long have you known?"

"Not long." Gail spoke softly, though without any attempt to dissemble, for which Ali appreciated her immensely. "Forel kept you a secret, and we had no idea he had succeeded in making a hybrid until I had to fit you with the mechanical arm."

"Why didn't you tell me then?"

Gail produced her bundle of tools and spread it out before her. "We couldn't. Not unless we succeeded today. Barron, give me the Sidallite."

"We're not supposed to do that here."

Ali let out a sigh. Good. They'd fulfilled the mission, at least.

"If we don't do it now, she'll die!" Gail picked up forceps, and a scalpel. "Ali, I'm sorry, but this will hurt."

Ali blinked.

Wait, *what?*

The tip of the scalpel dug into her chest. Ali screamed as it moved down, and she watched, horrified, as Gail opened her ribcage like a drawer. Beneath the fleshy exterior, wires and pumps worked in sputtering intervals, and sparks flew from certain junctions. The sensation of Gail's wrench tightening valves, of her portable blowtorch sealing tubes, was one of peculiar detachment, an echo of a feeling, almost there but not quite. It was as though Ali could only feel pain on a surface level – on the level where she looked human.

Barron moved to the door to keep watch. Ali shifted her eyes to the dead replicas in the room. "If I'm one of them, how come I'm alive, and they're not?"

"The Evolutionists have been trying for years to make an artificial human. The closest they got was the ninth ALIR replica, but even though it had a perfect human constitution, they couldn't get it to breathe. Something about their brains being unable to connect to their bodies." Gail gave the other ALIRs a pitying look. "Unlike the rest of the Church, Forel thought the answer to the problem lay in Mechanism. The Church gave him an ultimatum: stop trying to marry Mechanism with Evolutionism, or die.

"Not one to give in to demands, Forel changed schools and became one of us. A couple of years later, he showed up with you, claiming you to be his apprentice."

Ali's sight slowly regained its clarity when Gail tightened

another valve, and she no longer spat out oil when she asked, "Why keep me a secret from the Mechanists, then?"

"Paranoia, I'd wager. He didn't want to risk anyone reporting you to the Church. What matters is that he *did* make an artificial human. I can't say for sure how he did it, but from examining you that day I can make an educated guess." She tightened another valve on top of Ali's stomach, then put the wrench away and wiped the sweat from her forehead with the back of her hand. "To compensate for an artificial brain's inability to communicate with the rest of the body, he installed a controller to connect both. When that still wouldn't work, he started adding mechanical pieces to your body. Your bones are titanium; your eyes are a work of glass and microcameras – the same sort you can find in the crow imaging device; your lungs are self-healing steel mesh – he probably got that one from some lizard or starfish; your brain is mostly human, with high-speed processors attached. He had skin grow on you, covering all his alterations. But more importantly... Your heart is clockwork, of the finest I've seen, and with an added cavity meant for something he couldn't get his hands on."

"Sidallite," Ali completed.

"Yes." Gail extended an arm, and Barron deposited a cloth-covered bundle in her hand. "Once you were finished, he put you on the streets, and waited for an opportunity to re-recruit you. Any memories you have from before you became his apprentice are fictitious. Lines of code, telling you of events you never experienced. I'm also assuming he had to repeatedly, erm... *improve* you as you grew."

"Hurry up, Gail," Barron called. "More guards are coming."

The mechanic didn't even blink. "Lock the door, and prepare for sacrifice." With her tweezers, Gail unwrapped the Sidallite, a fist-sized rock that glowed violet, currents of aether spinning within its transparent shell.

"Sacrifice?" Ali muttered.

"The automaton you and Forel built was a decoy. The

Sidallite was always meant to go inside you." She picked up the rock with her tweezers, and, with her free hand, she tapped a button on Ali's clockwork heart, which sprung open with a loud click. "There's only one of us who needs to get out of here, and it's you."

At the door, Barron knelt with the guns and ammo he'd gathered from the fallen guards, and was in the process of barricading the entrance with the few tables and chairs in the room.

Ali chuckled, a bitter sound of disillusionment and regret. "So. I'm your weapon."

Gail gave her a despondent smile in return. "You're our weapon. You're also one of our bravest and brightest. Never forget that." She ran a hand across Ali's cheek, but the tender touch was quickly withdrawn. "I'm not completely certain about this either, but there's a chance you think and feel like a human because your heart's been empty all along. Once the Sidallite goes in, your body will conduct energy better. You won't need to sleep, or eat; you probably will stop feeling exhaustion, too."

A booming sound reverberated through the room as the forces outside banged against the steel door. Barron came to kneel beside them, a gun in each hand. He and Gail exchanged a nod, after which the mechanic turned to Ali.

"You'll shut down momentarily while the Sidallite takes hold – we'll protect you in the meantime." She held the rock in front of Ali's empty heart. "Ready?"

Ali looked from the Sidallite to her open chest. She was a thing, built in a tank, then enhanced. An instrument of destruction, made of curiosity and set upon the path of vengeance.

Perhaps her artificial origins were showing, because Ali couldn't find it within herself to care. She was who she was, hybrid replica or not. The last thing she could do was end the Church's madness, and make sure they never created anything like her again.

She held Gail's gaze. "Ready."

The mechanic nodded. The Sidallite fit perfectly in Ali's heart, which closed automatically as soon as Gail released the stone from the tweezers. The springs in her chest rotated, snapped –

Darkness.

As though in a dream, Ali floated.

How long...

Her muscles sputtered, her insides spun. Power surged through her, seeping into her limbs, her torso, her head.

... had she been...

She became impossibly hot. Smoke filled her throat, her mouth, coated her tongue with its taste of ash.

... in the dark?

Ali lurched into wakefulness with a gasp. Looking down at herself, she found her chest closed, her body stronger, her eyesight sharper. At her feet, Gail and Barron lay dead, she from a hole on the side of her head, him from a chest full of holes.

A noise from the door claimed her attention. A bullet made its way towards her, but she was so fast now, she had all the time in the world to step aside, avoiding it, and pick up a knife from the floor. She jumped towards the guards, the force behind her legs a surprise she swiftly mastered. With her newly gained speed, opening their throats didn't take Ali longer than a couple of breaths.

Evolutionists tried to stop her in the lower levels, bringing their guns, their metamorphosed creatures. None were a match for what she'd become, now that the Sidallite was in her chest, giving her infinite power.

No one could stop her from setting fire to the lower levels, eradicating the Church's plan to grow a living being within a tank.

No one could keep her from walking out the front door with a trail of bodies behind her.

And, more importantly, no one stopped her when she reached the Academia, and tore down the Evolutionist libraries, study rooms, quarters. Broken mirrors reflected her appearance: a girl, around eighteen, with eyes of shining purple, moving faster than the eye could follow.

At last, she reached the Provost's rooms – the old man screeched when he saw her, called her an abomination when he realised what she was.

Ali tossed him from the window, and watched as he crashed to the stones beneath.

Flames devoured the building around her. For a moment – and Ali found she could now think so many parallel thoughts in a single moment – she considered letting herself burn along with them. She was an abomination given life, as much an atrocity as the bird man and the feline women and the squid boy and the stone girl. She should join them in death, let herself become forgotten.

Yet, she could not.

If she did, the Church would rise again, would try to grow people from tanks again; and the Mechanists... they were settling for automatons for now, but how long until they, too, tried to replicate what Forel had done? How long until they tried to make another ALIR-VI?

So, Ali jumped from the Academia, and lost herself in the city. She sought the Mechanists afterwards once, telling them their plan was a success – and then, she disappeared, to never be seen again.

For hundreds of years after that, whenever a Mechanist or an Evolutionist tried to follow in Forel's footsteps they would disappear without a trace. Eventually, the research was abandoned; eventually, they stopped trying.

But Ali still watched over the city – and kept on watching until humanity rose to the skies and broke through the atmosphere. She watched as the Earth aged before her eyes, watched as the sun burned out and extinguished all life.

She didn't age. Time didn't affect machines, not even hybrids.

She couldn't die. The Sidallite was an indestructible source of limitless energy. At one point, when the madness of eternity raged at its highest, she tried to pluck it out of her chest. It would've been easier to move a mountain.

To take her revenge – so small, it seemed so small now – Ali had become immortal, with nothing to do but watch. And, occasionally, interfere.

She took to outer space, a passenger on the very last ship to leave her dead planet.

And she watched.

And watched.

And watched.

And, when humanity finally met its end, in a war against another species from another universe…

She kept on watching.

Diana Pinguicha is a Portuguese Young Adult fiction writer. She is known for helping authors improve their manuscripts and for giving advice on how to approach literary agents. She has given several writing workshops and taken part in panels at Portuguese SF&F events. In her story, "Heart of Stone", she mixes science fiction and steampunk, creating a page-turner which once more asks the question: 'What makes us human?'

NEWCON PRESS

Publishing quality Science Fiction, Fantasy, Dark Fantasy and Horror for twelve years and counting.

Winner of the 2010 'Best Publisher' Award from the European Science Fiction Society. Winner of numerous BSFA and BFS Awards.

Anthologies, novels, short story collections, novellas, paperbacks, hardbacks, signed limited editions, e-books... Why not take a look at some of our other titles?

To date we have published work by

Neil Gaiman, Brian Aldiss, Kelley Armstrong, Alastair Reynolds, Stephen Baxter, Christopher Priest, Tanith Lee, Bruce Sterling, Joe Abercrombie, Dan Abnett, Nina Allan, Rachel Armstrong, Neal Asher, Chris Beckett, Lauren Beukes, Aliette de Bodard, Eric Brown, Pat Cadigan, Ramsey Campbell, Becky Chambers, Storm Constantine, Paul Cornell, Hal Duncan, Jaine Fenn, Paul di Filippo, Jon Courtenay Grimwood, Peter F. Hamilton, Frances Hardinge, Dave Hutchinson, Emmi Itäranta, Gwyneth Jones, M. John Harrison, Nancy Kress, Yoon Ha Lee, Mark Lawrence, Sarah Lotz, Paul McAuley, Ian McDonald, Ken MacLeod, Ian R. MacLeod, Gail Z. Martin, Simon Morden, Stan Nicholls, Jeff Noon, Claire North, Sarah Pinborough, Robert Reed, Mike Resnick, Mercurio D. Rivera, Adam Roberts, Jane Rogers, Justina Robson, Stephanie Saulter, Robert Shearman, Michael Marshall Smith, Brian Stapleford, Charles Stross, Tricia Sullivan, E.J. Swift, Adrian Tchaikovsky, Steve Rasnic Tem, Lavie Tidhar, Lisa Tuttle, Ian Watson, Liz Williams, & more.

Join our mailing list to get advance notice of new titles, book launches and events, and receive special offers on books.

www.newconpress.co.uk

Origamy

Rachel Armstrong

"*Origamy* is a magnificent, glittering explosion of a book: a meditation on creation, the poetry of science and the insane beauty of everything. You're going to need this." **– Warren Ellis**

Mobius knows she isn't a novice weaver, but it seems she must re-learn the art of manipulating spacetime all over again. Encouraged by her parents, Newton and Shelley, she starts to experiment, and is soon traveling far and wide across the galaxy, encountering a dazzling array of bizarre cultures and races along the way. Yet all is not well, and it soon becomes clear that a dark menace is gathering, one that could threaten the very fabric of time and space and will require all weavers to unite if the universe is to stand any chance of surviving.

Rachel Armstrong is Professor of Experimental Architecture at Newcastle University and a 2010 Senior TED Fellow. A former medical doctor, she now designs experiments that explore the transition between inert and living matter and considers their implications for life beyond our solar system.

"*Origamy* crackles with a strange and brilliant energy, and folds the conventions of SF into beautiful new shapes. A rare and wonderful debut." **– Adam Roberts**

"Perhaps the most astonishing and original piece of SF I've read in a long, long while." **– Adrian Tchaikovsky**

"A visionary masterpiece. Science Fiction, Fantasy, science and poetry combine to create a lyric on life and death that spans the whole of creation. Delightful and mind-expanding. If you miss it you have missed one of the finest examples of literary art." **– Justina Robson**

2001: AN ODYSSEY IN WORDS
Edited by Ian Whates and Tom Hunter

An anthology of original fiction to honour the centenary of Sir Arthur C. Clarke's birth and act as a fund raiser for the Clarke Award. Every story is precisely 2001 words long.

2001 includes stories by 10 winners of the Arthur C. Clarke Award and 13 authors who have been shortlisted, as well as non-fiction by **Neil Gaiman, China Miéville** and Chair of Judges **Andrew M. Butler**.

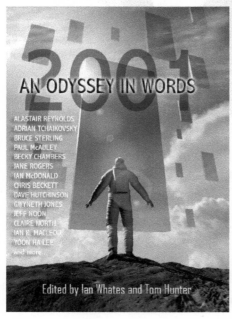

Cover art by Fangorn

Alastair Reynolds
Bruce Sterling
Gwyneth Jones
Adrian Tchaikovsky
Paul McAuley
Jane Rogers
Ian McDonald
Rachel Pollack
Chris Beckett
Jeff Noon
Colin Greenland
Becky Chambers
Claire North
Dave Hutchinson
Adam Roberts
Yoon Ha Lee
Ian R. MacLeod
Emmi Itäranta
Ian Watson
Liz Williams
& more

Twenty-seven stories from some of the biggest names in Science Fiction, honouring one of the genre's greats by exploring the limits of imagination.

Released by NewCon Press as a paperback and limited edition hardback.

OSUUSKUMMA is a Finnish co-operative publishing house specializing in all kinds of strange fiction — fantasy, sci-fi, horror, New Weird, steampunk, and the like. Recently we have branched out into international publications under "Osuuskumma International" to offer top-quality Finnish speculative fiction in languages other than Finnish.

www.osuuskumma.fi
www.finnishwriters.com

OSUUSKUMMA INTERNATIONAL

Kumma
Literary Agency

Editorial Divergência

Editorial Divergência is a Portuguese small press specialising in speculative fiction. Founded in 2013, it creates small print runs, with a focus on the quality of the finished book, promoting a honest relationship with its writers and readers.

www.divergencia.pt / geral@divergencia.pt

Immanion Press
Purveyors of Speculative Fiction

Venus Burning: Realms by Tanith Lee

Tanith Lee wrote 15 stories for the acclaimed *Realms of Fantasy* magazine. This book collects all the stories in one volume for the first time, some of which only ever appeared in the magazine so will be new to some of Tanith's fans. These tales are among her best work, in which she takes myth and fairy tale tropes and turns them on their heads. Lush and lyrical, deep and literary, Tanith Lee created fresh poignant tales from familiar archetypes.
ISBN 978-1-907737-88-6, £11.99, $17.50 pbk

A Raven Bound with Lilies by Storm Constantine

The Wraeththu have captivated readers for three decades. This anthology of 15 tales collects all the published Wraeththu short stories into one volume, and also includes extra material, including the author's first explorations of these beings. The tales range from the 'creation story' *Paragenesis*, through the bloody, brutal rise of the earliest tribes, and on into a future, where strange mutations are starting to emerge from hidden corners of the earth.
ISBN: 978-1-907737-80-0 £11.99, $15.50 pbk

The Lightbearer by Alan Richardson

Michael Horsett parachutes into Occupied France before the D-Day Invasion. Dropped in the wrong place, badly injured, he falls prey to two Thelemist women who have awaited the Hawk God's coming, attracts a group of First World War veterans who rally to what they imagine is his cause, is hunted by a troop of German Field Police, and has a climactic encounter with a mutilated priest who believes that Lucifer Incarnate has arrived...*The Lightbearer* is a unique gnostic thriller, dealing with the themes of Light and Darkness, Good and Evil, Matter and Spirit. ISBN 9781907737763 £11.99 $18.99

All these and more on our web site
Immanion Press
http://www.immanion-press.com
info@immanion-press.com

Lightning Source UK Ltd.
Milton Keynes UK
UKHW02f1221290618
324968UK00003B/63/P